Number

Fifteen

Tony McFadden

Beach Nut Press

DEDICATION

Find a charity that you can support that fights exploitation of women and child trafficking. There are many good ones out there.

Hagar Australia

A21

ZOE

DISCLAIMER

All characters in this book are fictitious. Any resemblance to real people is entirely coincidental.

This book is set in Australia, and written in Australia. It has Australian sayings and spellings.

And swearing. Lots and lots of swearing.

You have been warned.

ACKNOWLEDGMENTS

You're reading this due to the support of many beta-readers who have helped enormously.

.

Chapter One

Dan McGinnis turned his motorcycle into one of the 'McGinnis Investigations' spots, popped the kickstand and turned off the ignition. An echo of the throaty roar rapidly tailed off, replaced by a young woman's voice.

"Hey, boss. You're early today."

He pulled off his helmet and finger-combed back his hair. "You too, Kat. Piss the bed?"

She laughed. "Beautiful morning. I was up with the birds." Kat held up an envelope. "Any idea how I can get out of this?"

"Out of what?" He unzipped his jacket and flapped it for the cooling breeze. "Eight in the morning and already above thirty. It's going to be a hot summer."

She waved the envelope. "Jury summons."

Dan took it from her and extracted the letter. "Four week trial." He handed it back. "Could be worse."

"How?"

"I was called for a twenty-one week case a few years ago."

"You were on jury duty for five months? Jesus. Fuck that."

He shook his head and walked slowly toward the back entrance of the office. "I own a small business. I managed to get a deferral." He pointed at Kat. "You, though. You should sit on the panel." He held up his finger, interrupting an objection. "You won't lose any money. You get something like a hundred a day for jury duty. I'll make up the difference."

"Yeah, but jury duty," she said.

Dan stopped and faced her. "You're what, twenty-five, right?"

She crossed her arms. "Yeah?"

"So maybe step up and perform some civic duty. You'll enjoy it. Learn a bit about the law, too." He sighed and continued walking. "It's almost a week away. They might not even need you." He lifted his hand to enter the code in the keypad by the door and stopped. "Kat?"

"What?"

"When did you get here this morning?"

"Same time as you. What's going on?"

Dan stood to one side. Four of the digits on the keypad were covered in drying blood. A smear on the doorframe was partially covered by the closed door. Dan took out a pen and used it to enter the code. "This isn't that old. It's still not fully dry. In this heat it would be crusted over in minutes." He pulled the door open.

She pointed at the stairs up to the third floor. "Steady flow of drops. Whoever it is, they were hurt bad."

"And still up there."

Kat slipped her mobile phone out of her back pocket. "I'll call the cops."

Dan held out his hand, stopping her. "Let's see what's up there first."

He walked carefully up the three flights, at the edge of each tread, keeping clear of the blood splatter. "Careful."

"Brand new Converse, boss. Don't worry." She followed in Dan's steps until they reached their offices.

Blood was smeared across the door. The doorknob was bloody, and the door part way open. Dan pushed it with his foot and stood back while it slowly revealed blood streaks leading across the tiled floor into the kitchen area.

He followed the blood trail. A large man was face down in a pool of hardening blood in front of the sink. His ragged breathing was punctuated by a gurgling sound on each exhale.

Kat dropped to her knees and took him by the shoulder. "Andy?"

"Don't move him." Dan dialled 0-0-0 on his phone, put it on speaker mode and placed it on the counter.

"You've dialled Triple Zero Emergency Services. Do you need police, fire or ambulance?"

"Police and Ambo." Dan squatted by Andy. "I found one of my

employees in the office. He's breathing, but bleeding bad." He gave them the address. "As fast as you can." He dropped the call.

"He's conscious, Dan." Kat leaned her head near Andy's. "He's saying something." She put her phone on voice recorder and held it by his mouth. "What is it, Andy? Who did this?"

He rolled to the side and wheezed something before dropping back onto his face.

"What did he say?"

Kat shook her head and turned off the recorder. "I don't know. He's going to be okay, right?"

"Wait at the front for the Ambo. Send the cops up as soon as they show." He kneeled beside Andy. "Go." He watched Kat as she ran from the kitchen. Her footfalls echoed down the front stairs.

"What in the hell have you gotten yourself into, mate?" He rested a hand on Andy's back, the shallow breaths barely moving it. He reached his phone off the counter and sent a group text to the rest of his team and sat on the floor with his back against the cupboards. The blood under Andy's head was congealing. His dark hair was matted and his face and neck were a blotchy deep purple.

Andy was large. He'd left the SAS years earlier, but kept up the training regimen. He was hard, vicious and took a step backward for nobody.

And he had been brutalised.

His phone rang. "Are they here yet, Kat?"

"I can hear the sirens. Are you giving him CPR?"

"He's breathing. I'm not going to move him. I don't know what the damage is."

"They're here. Up in a sec."

He stayed beside his friend, listening to the commotion coming up the front stairs, resting his hand on Andy's back, making sure he kept breathing.

Kat led paramedics into the kitchen. "He's on the floor, over there."

Dan moved out of their way. "His breathing is shallow. A lot of blood loss."

"We've got it from here."

Senior Constable Warren Peters followed the paramedics in. "What happened, Dan?"

"Wazza, glad it's you." He stepped out of the way so Peters could see Andy. "We found him like that."

"That's Andy? How long has he been here?"

"How in the hell would I know?"

One of the paramedics looked up at Peters. "State of the blood, I'd say between one and two hours."

"What's the damage?"

The para shook her head. "Hard to detail. Multiple broken bones, a collapsed lung. Full inventory at the hospital."

"We'll be right behind you," said Dan.

"I've got some questions, Dan." Peters pulled a small notepad from his shirt pocket. "When did you find Andy?"

Dan watched the paramedics manoeuvre the gurney to the top of the stairs. "This morning, not even half an hour ago. When I got here."

Kat watched him watch them. "I'll go with them. Come when you can." She followed the paramedics as they carefully navigated their way out.

Dan blew out a slow breath. "Thanks, Kat. Down the back steps, Peters. Be careful."

Peters surveyed the mess in the kitchen. "Make sure this doesn't get cleaned up until Crime Scene techs get here." He pointed at the back stairs. "Show me."

Dan walked down the stairs, keeping at the edge of the treads. "Blood splatter along the stairway." He pushed the back door open with the toe of his boot. "Come outside."

Peters followed. "Is his car out here?"

Dan scanned the parking lot and shook his head. "He must have walked here. Blood on the keypad and smeared on the door."

"Already saw that."

"I'm going to block off the parking lot until the CS crew has a run through it." Peters took a deep breath and leaned forward, looking Dan directly in the eyes. "Leave this one to us, Danny. Police matter. I know you'll feel an overwhelming urge to find whoever did this to Andy, so repress it."

"Or?"

"Come on, Dan. Let me do my job."

"You really think I'm not going to have my team all over this? Stay out of my way and I'll stay out of yours." Dan rhythmically clenched his jaw muscles. "Seriously, mate. This crosses so many lines I've lost count."

Peters rested a hand on Dan's shoulder. "I'll let you know what I find out. You should probably head to the hospital."

Dan shook his head. "Beryl, Stew and Terry are coming here. I need to let them know what's going on. Andy is going to be in surgery for a couple of hours." He paused. "I'm going to move my bike out front before you lock this place down."

He parked in a 2 hour spot in front of the office and followed Beryl in.

"What happened?" she asked. Her close cropped grey hair was still damp.

He walked up the front stairs beside her, their footsteps echoing off the concrete walls. "Don't know. Kat and I found him in the kitchen when we came in. Bashed hard. Didn't look good."

"Kat's upstairs?"

"She went with him to the hospital. He was breathing, but…" He rubbed his face. "Andy is the toughest fucker I've ever met. Yet he was pulverised."

They reached the top of the stairs. Stew, looking like the solid rock that he was, and Terry, trying to look tough, but failing, met them at the door.

"What was Andy working on?" Stew was in his mid-fifties, but hard as the rock he'd throw around making jetties and sea walls for the stupidly rich on the north shore. His arms were crossed, biceps like small boulders. "He didn't tell me."

"Didn't tell me either." Terry had the build of a twenty-seven-year old audio/video tech. But he was as tense as Stew. He repeatedly clenched and unclenched his fists.

Crime scene techs were in the kitchen, with the path to the back door taped off. Dan watched them for a minute, then directed Beryl, Stew and Terry to the conference room. "We need to set some parameters, then I'm going to the hospital. Everything else goes to the back burner."

Beryl nodded. "I'll call the active cases, tell them that there will be some delays."

"Thanks." He furrowed his brow. "How many?"

"Active? Just the two. Both small."

He took a deep breath. "Okay." He sat at the head of the conference table. The others sat around it, leaning forward.

"Andy had asked for a week of personal time to investigate something. Didn't tell me what it was, and I got the impression it was truly personal. Whatever it was, it ended up with him in our kitchen, face down in a pool of his blood." He looked at the faces around the table. All of them hard, angry, looking for some sort of revenge.

"Don't let emotions rule. Anger invites mistakes, in judgement and in tactical awareness. Go to the gym and beat the fuck out of a heavy bag if you have to, then come back and be rational. We're going to find out what happened, and when we've dragged whoever did this into our office, then we'll mete out the appropriate punishments."

"What was he working on?"

He pushed back his chair and stood. "See what you can find out from his files. I'm going to the hospital. I'll let you know when he's out of surgery."

Kat met him at the entrance to A&E at Campbelltown Hospital.

"What's the news?"

"He's still under the knife. Concussion, four broken ribs on his right side, collapsed lung, multiple broken fingers, nose…" She wiped away a tear. "He'll live, but someone did a number on him."

"More than one someone. He's never lost a one-on-one fight. I don't suppose he woke up and said anything that might shed any light on this?"

She sniffed and shook her head.

Dan pulled her in for a hug. "He's tough. He'll get through this."

She nodded and pulled away. "The doctor is coming."

Dan turned and half a smile cracked his face. "Doctor Jane."

"Doctor Golding, to you. What in the hell happened to Andy?"

"We're going to find out. How is he doing?"

"Concussion, some broken bones. He's tough. He'll be in here for a couple of days. You can come by if you want, but he won't be in any shape to have a conversation for at least another couple of hours."

"Thanks. I'll tell Stew you said hi."

She blushed. "He's going to get himself in trouble over this, isn't he?"

"Knowing Stew, probably."

Jane chewed her lip in thought. "He contacted Mac a couple of days ago, asked for some help."

"Who?"

"Andy."

"No, who is Mac?"

"My ex, a PI up on the Central Coast." She shook her head. "Don't know what about."

"You have a number for him?"

Jane grabbed Dan's hand and wrote a mobile number on it.

Dan held his palm toward him and used his other hand to add the contact to his phone. "Thanks. I'll reach out."

"Tell him I said hi. Don't worry about Andy. He's in good hands."

Dan watched her leave and sat in a plastic chair in the waiting room. He patted the chair beside him. "Are you as tired as I am?"

"Stress'll do that to you." Kat leaned her head back and closed her eyes. "I think I figured out what he said when we showed up."

"What?"

"He gurgled something. I recorded it." She took out her phone. "Listen to this."

She played the voice memo, leaning in to listen, her head almost touching Dan's. There were discrete syllables coming out of the recording, but mostly gurgling.

"I'm not making anything out."

"Really?" Kat played it again.

"Really. Tell me what you're hearing."

"If I tell you, that's all you'll hear. Won't be able to unhear it."

"Play it again."

Dan cocked his head and listened. He motioned for her to play it again and closed his eyes, straining to understand.

"One syllable, followed by two syllables." He cocked his head. "Again." He steepled his fingers and rested his forehead on them. *"Please. Find her."*

"Exactly what I thought," said Kat. "Any idea who *her* is?"

Chapter Two

Dan caught a glimpse of Beryl powering in through the A&E doors and held a hand up to Kat. "Hang on." He stood. "Beryl, over here."

She strode with grim determination and sat on the other side of Kat. She took her by the hand, matronly and mother-like. "You okay? Rough thing to walk in on."

Kat looked past her. "Yeah, I'll be okay. Where are the others?"

"Terry is holding down the fort and Stew stormed out of the office like whiskey was on sale. Don't know where he went." She fussed with her slacks. "How's Andy?"

"Should be able to talk to him in two or three hours. He's out of commission for a while," said Dan. "Really no point hanging around here. We've got work to do."

Beryl looked at the packed A&E waiting room and nodded. "Yeah. Depressing place."

"Beryl, where had Andy been the last couple of days?"

"No clue. Off the clock. Said he had something to sort out." She pushed herself up out of her chair. "This discussion is for the office. See you in five." Kat followed her out, giving him a wave over her shoulder.

Dan watched them leave then dug out his phone. He called Mac as he walked. It rang out to voicemail.

"This is Mac Durridge. I'm not in the office. Do it at the beep."

He didn't do it at the beep. He jammed the phone in his pocket and climbed on his bike.

It was only a five minute ride. It didn't give Dan much time to think. Andy had been only on the periphery of work for the past week or so. And business had been light. It was like that. Private Investigation services were feast or famine. The feasts more than made up for the famine, and if you fought against the low points and tried to force work you'd just drive yourself crazy. It was cyclic. It always came around.

And in the slow periods he didn't expect any of his team to be in the office nine to five. They never kept those kinds of hours anyway. Which explained why Dan hadn't really registered the fact that Andy hadn't been around.

Beryl and Kat were looking at the blood on the doorframe and keypad when he parked. The crime scene techs were packing up, tearing down tape.

"There are companies that do this sort of work, Beryl. Don't do the cleaning yourself."

Beryl threw him a half smile. "Not an idiot, pup. I called a cleaner before I went to the hospital. They'll do the stairs and the kitchen." She pointed at the keypad. "I can do this." She adjusted her purse on her shoulder. "We need to talk. Terry is upstairs."

"Stew?"

She shook her head. "Not back. It doesn't look like we'll see him again today."

He walked up the stairs, stepping over the dried blood stains. "How long before I get a call to bail him out, do you think? Impetuous old man. Like a bloody teenager."

"I wonder where he gets that from?" Beryl pushed past him and surveyed the kitchen. The cleaning crew was finishing up under Terry's watchful eye. "They doing a good job?" The crew was two middle-aged men in full crime scene tech bunny suits, formerly white but now aged with old brown blood stains and yellowed sweat stains. They glanced up at Terry and kept cleaning the floor.

Terry nodded. "What are we going to do about this?"

"We're going to talk about it in the conference room, not in front of them," said Beryl, leading them in.

They didn't sit. Kat stood at the window, arms crossed, looking out over the back parking lot. Terry leaned against the wall and Beryl paced.

"Okay." Dan took a deep breath and sat. "What do we know?'"

They kept their thoughts to themselves for a minute. Dan let it soak. His was a tight-knit crew, and one of the team getting taken out hurt all of them.

Kat spoke first. "It had to be nearby. He was too beat up to travel far, I don't care how tough he is. And he made it up the stairs." She shrugged and sat at the table. "So somewhere around here. Security videos might show something."

Dan nodded. "Do *any* of you know what he was looking into?"

"Not really," said Terry. "Said it was a personal thing. Not billable." He sat. "Something happened about a week ago."

"That's when the Barron case closed. Been slow since then," said Beryl.

Kat held up a finger. "And that thing he said. To find her, whoever she is."

Beryl held up a hand. "Hang on. What's this?"

"He gurgled something when we found him." She dug out her phone. "Listen." She played the recording a couple of times.

Beryl leaned forward. "Find her? What do you know about his family, Dan?"

"His parents live in Joondalup in WA. No brothers or sisters that I know of. We've all been to his house, no wife or kids."

"I'll contact his parents," said Beryl. "See if there's a female family member missing."

"Thanks. Terry, get his phone from the hospital and get anything off of it that you can. Beryl, did he use any surveillance equipment?"

"Not that I know of, but I'll check."

"Kat, you and I are going to get what we can from cameras around here." Dan clenched his fists and rested them on the table. "If any of you hear from Stew, tell him to call me. I don't care what time of the day it happens to be, or where he is."

Chapter Three

Samuel Prescott stood on the back deck of his Vaucluse home, cup of coffee in one hand and his phone in the other. They were behind schedule, by about seven hours. An inexcusable situation.

The Manly ferry pushed through the water in front of him, heading toward Circular Quay, from right to left, the upper deck full. It was a warm day. He saluted the commuters with his coffee cup. None of them noticed. That suited him fine. Under the radar was best.

His young wife swam lazy laps in their pool. He watched her lithe form slice through the water and smiled. Rich was nice.

His phone buzzed. It was an unknown number. "Hello."

"Boss."

"You're late. What in the hell is going on?"

"There were complications. Couldn't get into port when we thought we could."

"Bad weather?" Prescott clenched his fist tight around the phone. "That excuse is getting old."

"No, no. I understand it was smooth sailing. Like a cruise ship."

"So what, then?"

"Our contact at the port had their shift changed. We didn't find out until it was almost too late. We're good, though. We cancelled our berthing slot and got a new one."

Prescott placed his coffee cup on a coaster on the glass-topped table. He took a deep breath. "So how in the FUCK is this supposed to work? When are they docking?"

"Around 6 pm tomorrow."

"In BROAD FUCKING DAYLIGHT? Are you really that stupid?" His wife looked up from the pool. He waved her away. This was none of her business. "Abort this shipment. Permanently. You'll carry whatever costs you've incurred. Get it done right the next time."

"Hang on. Not necessary."

"I'm not taking the risk. If you're too stupid to realise the risk, there's nothing I can do for you. My name comes up, even once, when you're arrested, and I'll have you killed, but not before I kill your family, slowly, while you watch. Abort it."

"No, listen to me. We've got secure transfer to transport. Out of sight. Nobody but our contact at the port will be involved. Then a quick run to the safe house just outside Campbelltown where we lay low. Then it's just like normal."

"Port Kembla to Campbelltown is how far?"

"Forty minutes. Maybe forty-five. We'll stick to the speed limit, easy flow. Nothing stupid."

Prescott scratched his chin in thought. "Same deal. My name comes up, you're out, permanently."

"Yeah, whatever. Fucking hell, man. This shipment is worth a mill, easy. A couple of pieces are collector's items."

"I know. Don't fuck up."

He closed off the call, dropped the phone on the table and picked up his coffee. He took a sip and winced. It was lukewarm.

"Everything okay, Sammy?" Lizzie was lithe, Asian and thirty years younger than him. And high maintenance.

"It always is." He leaned forward, getting into her face. "And it doesn't concern you, right?"

"Right. Whatever. I don't care." She waved her hand generally around the property. "Especially if I've got all this."

Prescott grabbed her by the arm. "Especially? You keep it low-key under ANY circumstances. Understand?"

Lizzie squinted up at her husband. "Right-o. Understood, Sir." She saluted with her free hand, pulled her arm free and headed back to the pool. "Whatever, babe."

He watched her settle into a chaise lounge and start rubbing sunscreen on her arms. "Time for a change, I think."

Prescott sat at the table and tapped the edge of his cup. He grabbed his phone, scrolled through his contacts and placed a call. "Christophe, I need you to push the auction out by twenty-four hours."

"That's going to be dif-"

"I don't give a fuck if it's going to be difficult. This is why you get paid. Push it. The product is top shelf and the customers will wait."

"The venue is - "

"Did you hear me tell you I didn't give a fuck? I don't give a fuck. Push it." He hung up. It would be pushed.

Chapter Four

The cleaners had finished the stairs, were out of their bunny suits and loading their equipment into their old panel van when Beryl walked down the back stairs with a critical eye. "Not bad." She handed one of the men a card. "Send the invoice directly to me and I'll make sure it's paid promptly."

He smiled, tucked the card in his shirt pocket and left.

She walked back up the stairs and sniffed. A strong bleach smell overpowered everything else. She wrinkled her nose and joined the others in the conference room.

"This place needs a good airing out."

Dan stood and pushed his chair into the conference table. "Let's get out of here and get some food. I'll buy."

"The new chicken place," said Terry.

"I'm going to the hospital to check in on Andy."

Dan looked at his watch. "You might have a wait, Beryl. I doubt he's awake yet."

"I'll wait then."

"Not hungry?"

"Hospital food will do for now."

Dan frowned. "You're worried about him."

Beryl snorted and headed down the back stairs. "Lock up when you leave."

Dan watched as she slowly walked down the stairs.

"She seems more concerned than usual," said Kat.

Dan glanced at her and nodded. "You've only been here a few months."

"Six."

"Right. When have you ever seen Andy laid out like that?"

"Not ever, I don't think, but I kind of assumed that in this business it would happen with some regularity."

"Not Andy. Let's get some food."

Terry stood and stretched. "Heard from Stew?"

Dan held up his phone and shook his head. "Right to voicemail."

"Could have told you that. I've been trying to track his phone and it's been offline for five hours now. I'm famished. Is the new chicken place the one beside the pool supply shop?"

"Opposite. Across the street. Near that Asian market."

"It better be good. I'm starving."

Kat looked at his thin frame. "Where does it go, Ter? It's going to catch up with you one day."

"I'll enjoy it while I can. Can we go, already?"

The three walked the two blocks to the new shop, Dan in the middle with Kat and Terry on either side.

"I've been wracking my brains and I can't think of any past cases that would snap back on us hard enough to get him beat like that," said Dan. "If we're going to find who did this we're going to have to take his personal life apart. Had any luck with his phone?"

Terry shook his head. "Haven't got it yet. Still at the hospital with all of his other personal effects."

"How are you going to unlock it?" asked Kat. "Use his thumb at the hospital?"

Dan laughed. "Andy refuses to use any biometrics. No fingerprints, no facial recognition, no voiceprints. Nothing."

"A bit paranoid."

Terry shrugged. "It works for him, right? Can't get into his phone without his help. Exactly as he intended." He narrowed his eyes in thought. "But I'll figure it out."

"You will." Dan held open the door to Campbelltown Chooks. "Let's get some food."

The restaurant was almost empty. A dozen or so dark wooden tables were spread throughout the low ceilinged establishment. Mahogany walls were decorated with alternating paintings of outback Australia and gilt-framed mirrors.

An elderly couple sat at a table for two near the back, eating their dinner and conversing in hushed tones. A middle-aged server at the front, near the pay station, picked up three menus and escorted them to a table.

"Anything to drink first?" His Asian accent was strong. He wore a white shirt with an open collar and a black vest. The edge of a tattoo was visible at the end of his left sleeve and on his chest, peeking above the open collar.

Terry looked at Dan. "Boss is buying. Pint of 50 Lashes for me."

"Water's fine," said Kat. She took the menu, opened it, but didn't look at the contents. "So Andy *never* gets beat up?"

Terry chuckled. "Andy would be on the receiving end of a scrap on a weekly basis, up to about a couple of years ago. Not so often now, but the results are still the same. Or they were until today. He'd get a bruise or two, the odd black eye, but never walloped like what happened today."

"So…" Kat looked at the menu. "Chicken parm looks good."

"Andy is ex-military. Trained hand-to-hand combat. Like, he trained people in hand-to-hand. One person didn't do this to Andy. It would have been a crowd. A very motivated crowd. We should check if there were any other admittances to the hospital."

Kat shook her head. "I've been thinking about that. He was dumped out back."

"What makes you say that?"

"Be a lot more blood in the parking lot if that's where the fight was. And he was too banged up to travel far." She held up a finger. "And even if he *had* travelled, there'd -"

"- be a trail of blood to the door from beyond the street, not just in the parking lot," finished Terry.

"Right." Kat scowled. "What he said."

"Valid point. You and I are checking CCTV tomorrow morning. We have cameras in the back. The restaurant beside us does, also."

"Why not tonight?"

"Nothing to gain. Half the shops will be closed and we won't be doing ourselves, or Andy, any good by pulling an all-nighter going over what little video we collect. Get some food in you first, get some rest, fresh run at it in the morning. What are you going to have?"

They ordered their meals and ate in relative silence. Dan watched the two youngest members of his team, deep in thought, trying to figure out what to do next. They were young, very smart, dedicated and keen.

He picked at his chicken caesar salad and looked around the new place. It was still quiet. The elderly couple was finishing off a shared dessert and coffee. Nobody else had come in.

"Seem kinda dead to you?"

Terry looked up from his chicken kiev. "What's that?"

"This place. We're going to be the only ones in here as soon as nan and gramps are finished their ice cream."

"It's new."

"Yeah. Should be packed with locals trying out the new place. Bet it folds before the end of the month."

Kat looked around. "No bet. Too bad. The food is pretty good."

A young girl in a white shirt and black vest came out through the kitchen doors and hovered near their table. "*Chbhaey*? Finished?" She pointed at Terry's plate.

"What? No. Not yet. Thanks."

Kat passed her almost empty plate to the girl. "Here you go." She looked at the girl's wrists, and then at Dan. He gave her a slight shake of his head. She nodded and held up her glass. "Could I get some more water, please?

The girl took her glass and refilled it and handed it back, then disappeared back into the kitchen.

"You see that?" asked Kat.

Dan crunched on a crouton and nodded. "Yeah. Bruised wrist. Not our business, Kat. We can't save everyone."

"I don't like it."

"That's good. You shouldn't. Maybe we take a another look in after this Andy business is resolved, okay?"

"Can't wait." She continued staring at the kitchen door behind which the girl had disappeared.

"Kat? No fights tonight." Dan rested a hand on her arm. "We'll come back."

"If you don't, I sure as hell will."

Dan picked at his salad. "Whoever took out Andy didn't need to dump him. It was a message, like they thought we were all involved in whatever he was looking into." He popped another crouton in his mouth. "So be careful. If they know who he was and where he worked, they'll know all of us."

Kat toyed with her water. She wiped some condensation off the glass and used it to clean food remnants from her fingertips. "We have a Dropbox service where case files are stored, right? A central hub so we can all access the latest info. You think maybe Andy opened a new file?"

Dan shrugged. "Hard to say. He has ironclad rules about keeping personal and professional separate. Six years I've known him and I know very little of his life. And that's his business."

"I'll check," said Terry. He opened an app on his phone and logged into Dropbox. He scrolled through the folders. "Nothing obvious. Unless he hid it. Which he could do."

The man who seated them hovered by the table. "Would you care for desserts?"

Dan waved him away. "We're good. Bring the bill, please."

Terry watched him leave. "I wanted some ice cream."

"We've got work to do." Dan took the bill, checked the total, and handed the man two fifty dollar notes. "Keep the change."

The server smiled and bowed and watched them leave.

They talked as they walked.

"I'm heading back to the office." Dan checked the time on his phone. "It's after seven. No obligation for you two to come back with me. We can pick this up in the morning."

"I'll help any way I can."

Terry nodded. "Me too. Easier to find a hidden folder on a big monitor than on my phone."

Kat frowned. "Right. That makes no sense."

"You wouldn't understand."

"I will fucking cut you if you treat me like a tech dummy."

Dan got between them. "Enough. I can never tell if you two are really fighting or just fucking around." He slowed as they reached the office. "Division of labour to keep things moving. I'll see what I can find out about Andy's past, Terry, you check Dropbox for any hidden files. Kat, check the electronics inventory. See if there's anything missing that might provide a clue as to what he was up to."

He took the stairs two at a time, Terry and Kat in his wake. "We're not going to be here all night. Do what we have to do. Meet in my office in an hour for a debrief."

Terry flashed up his laptop and routed the display to a large monitor. He scrolled through the folders in the shared drive. Did some quick calculations. The used space was half a gig larger than the sum of the individual folders. Something was hidden there. 500 megabytes worth of something. Not a large amount, compared to other cases they'd logged, but substantial enough to not be a rounding error. He scribbled some figures on a piece of paper and made his way to Dan's office.

Dan exercised every bit of background source data he had. It felt strange doing deep dives on one of his team, and not on a dirtbag who'd skipped bail. "Where are you, Stew?" he muttered. "You're a lot better at this shit than I am."

Terry poked his head in. "I just checked his phone. Still offline."

He dropped the paper on Dan's desk and sat in the chair across from him. "There's a hidden folder on the share drive. It's implied, anyway. The numbers don't add up. I'd need to log in as Andy to access it."

Dan picked up the paper. "Half a gig? Nothing to sneeze at."

"About right for a single user case. Any idea what his password is?"

"You're supposed to figure that out, kid."

Terry leaned back, balancing the chair on its two back legs. "I will. Faster if you knew it."

"No way in hell he'd tell anyone. And pretty sure he uses two-factor."

Terry rubbed an eye with the heel of his hand. "You're probably right." He checked the time. "I'm going to pop over to the hospital, see how he's doing, get his phone."

"If Beryl is still there, tell her to go home. It's getting late."

Terry nodded and pushed himself to his feet. "Yeah. Day's getting longer than I like it to be."

Kat pushed past him as he left. She took his chair. "There are two wireless microphones, the really good camera and a couple of remote pinhole cameras missing from inventory. Next to nothing, really."

"This isn't getting us very far." His mobile phone rang. He looked at the display and answered. "You forget something, Terry?"

"The cops are out here. Want to talk to you."

Chapter Five

Dan stood and looked out his office window down on the street. Two marked police cars and Senior Constable Warren Peters' unmarked sedan were parked outside the front entrance. "We've got company. Play nice."

Kat stood beside him. "Do I have to stay? Could sneak out the back and they'd never know I was here."

The door at the bottom of the stairs opened and a parade of footsteps echoed their way up. "Don't think you'll have the opportunity." He left his office and met them at the door.

Peters shook Dan's hand. "Hey, mate. Got some more questions."

"It's kinda late."

"It's kinda important."

"Okay. Into the conference room."

Terry, Kat and Dan sat on one side of the table and Warren and two uniforms sat across from them.

"Can I get you boys some coffee?"

Peters held up a hand. "No, I don't think we'll be long." He checked his watch. "What are you doing here with a team at 7:30?"

"Normal workday for us, Wazza. You know that. You wouldn't have popped by if you didn't expect to see us here."

"You, maybe. Not the youngsters."

Dan shrugged. "Tying up loose ends."

Peters flipped open a notebook, fished a pen out of his shirt pocket and looked up at Dan. "Same here." He checked a note. "Any idea who might have bashed Andy?"

"I wouldn't be here, sitting on my arse, if I did, mate. I'd be out doing something about it." He tapped his phone to wake up the screen and checked the time. "And I'm wasting my time, sitting on my arse, talking to you."

Peters looked at one of the uniforms, then at Kat and Terry. "We're thinking that some of your prior cases may be coming back to bite. You've had some tricky ones, right?"

"Nobody involved in any cases we worked would be able to do Andy like that. We're mostly missing persons and surveillance for scorned wives."

"Mostly. You've recently had some interactions with some bikies from down south. And," he checked his notes, "there was that Rand Murray thing recently. He had some muscle that ended up in the hospital. Maybe they came back to get some licks in."

"I wouldn't know anything about those guys ending up in the hospital."

Terry snorted, trying to keep a laugh in. Kat kicked his foot.

Peters scribbled a note. "We can't tie you to their assault, and I really don't give a shit who did it, but we need to look at the possibility."

Dan shook his head. "You've met Andy, right? Former special forces, trained other special forces in hand-to-hand, never, ever lost a fight? That Andy?" He rested his hands, palm down on the table. "Whoever did this, whoever put Andy in the hospital, there had to be a lot of them, and they had to be hard." He leaned forward. "You run into a group of really hard guys lately?"

"We're investigating, Dan. That's why we're here." He flipped back a couple of pages. "Tell me about him."

"Andy? Electronics genius. Ex-SAS. Fitter than any three of us combined. Brains and brawn."

"Family? Close friends? Enemies?"

"His parents are in WA. No siblings or steady girlfriends, as far as I know."

"Boyfriends?"

"None of them either. A loner."

"What did he do for you?"

"You mean what *does* he do for me? Muscle, the odd time it's needed, and surveillance. He's very good at surveillance."

"And you have no idea what he was working on." It wasn't a

question. Peters stared intently at Dan's face.

"We're in the middle of a welcomed lull. Andy was free-lancing something on his own. Trust me. I have no clue what it was."

"Maybe it was racial."

Dan squinted. "What?"

"He's Aboriginal, isn't he?"

"Yeah. Wudjari." Dan shook his head. "We've been working out of this place for almost a decade. He's never had a problem. Jesus. Look out the window. Pick a colour. They're all out there.

Peters flipped his notepad shut. "As soon as you figure out what he was up to, call me, okay?"

Dan took a deep breath and looked to his right at Kat and Terry. "I thought that was your job, Peters. I guess we'll handle this on our own."

"That would be interfering with a police investigation, Dan. You'd lose your licence. Look, we've known each other since high school. I don't want to make this a big deal, but if you get in our way, it will be. It's an official police investigation. Stay out of our way. Got it?"

Dan sucked air in between his teeth. "Thanks for stopping by, Senior Constable. I'll be locking up soon. Please see yourselves out."

"Be careful, mate." Peters stood and nodded at the two with him. "We'll be in touch."

Dan waited until their boots made it to the bottom of the stairs and he heard the door slam shut behind them before he spoke. "Fuck that."

"Can you really lose your licence?" asked Kat.

Dan pushed away from the table and stood. "Blowing hot air. Don't stop what you're doing. Let me worry about it." He saw Terry check his watch. "I mean, stop for tonight. It's getting late. But pick it up tomorrow." He held up an index finger, then put it to his lips. "Shh."

The front door creaked open, then slammed closed. He heard the 'snick' of the deadbolt then footsteps coming up into the office. He stood near the door and peered out, tense. He saw who reached the top of the stairs and relaxed.

"We're in here, Beryl." He sat back at the table and waited for her to enter.

"What were the cops doing here?" She dropped her purse on the table and sat in the seat Peters had recently vacated.

"Probably exactly what you think."

"Peters tell you to keep your nose out?"

"Yeah. How did you know he was here?"

"Are you going to?"

"You know me better than that. How did you know?"

"Got back here about five minutes ago. Saw the cars and decided to wait until they left." She grimaced. "I'd be shackled in the back of one of those cars if I was here when they told you to shut it down. No goddamned way."

"How's Andy?"

"Briefly woke. Moaned something about 'those fuckers' and

faded. He's on some really good pain meds. He'll be knocked out for a good while." She nodded toward Terry and Kat. "The youngsters find anything yet?"

"He took two wireless microphones, the really good camera and a couple of remote pinhole cameras." Kat shrugged. "Nothing that records and stores, so we're truly no farther ahead knowing that."

"He does have a Dropbox folder we can't get into," said Terry. "Half a gig worth. I'm working on it."

"He uses two-factor."

"I know." Terry held out his hand.

Beryl dug through her purse and smiled at Terry. She extracted a flip-phone and tossed it at Terry. "Old school. Barely a smart phone. 2FA will be a text message."

"What's the password?"

"There is none, kid. There's no need for one. He memorised phone numbers and never added them as contacts. Not really much more technically advanced than an ink pen."

Terry checked the message log. "Good security protocol. All messages, incoming and outgoing, are deleted."

Beryl looked across the table at the three of them. "So that's it? Not much of anything."

"Just starting. Full court press tomorrow." Dan rested his elbows on the table and steepled his fingers. "How's he doing?"

Beryl scratched the back of her head and let out a long, slow breath. "He's tough. You, Dan, would be out of commission for a couple of weeks. Terry would be dead."

"Hey."

"Shut up, kid. The adults are talking." She briefly smiled at him and continued. "Three fractured and two broken ribs. That's nothing. The broken ones are held in place with little bits of wire. Then there's the fractured patella. I understand that hurts like a son of a bitch, but doesn't impact mobility much. Concussion brought on by a fractured skull. That's the bit they worried about the most. He was lucky, though. No swelling, no brain bleeds and nothing to worry about in the head department." She paused for a second. "Was that it? No. Collapsed lung, but only a by-product of the fractured ribs. Dislocated shoulder, but that's been popped back into place. Looks like he'll live."

Beryl narrowed her eyes. "So let's get started. What's he been doing for the past week? Who is the 'her' he's looking for? What army managed to take him out?"

"We've got the same questions, too late to do anything about it." Dan stretched. "He'll live. You're right. And he'll heal. We get a red mist over our eyes and rush headlong into something before we know what we're getting into, we'll, at the very least, end up in a bed beside Andy." He rubbed an eye with the heel of his hand. "I'm tired. We'll reconvene in the morning. If you get here before me, we're going to tear apart whatever he was up to over the past five days. Terry, devote your time to Dropbox, Kat, check neighbours' security videos. Beryl, recheck inventory and see if there might be anything he signed out that transmits." He yawned. "But tomorrow. Not tonight."

Kat opened her mouth to say something. "No, Kat. Andy is in good hands. He'll be fine. Go home and get some sleep."

She stood and pocketed her phone. "Wasn't going to say anything about Andy. I was going to say, see you tomorrow. See you tomorrow."

Kat let the front door swing shut behind her and walked toward the chicken place. It was still a warm night. She took a short cut through the parking lot at the back of the restaurant. There were only a few cars and a couple of pickup trucks reflecting the distant street lights off their windscreens. A warm breeze kept the smell from the large, wheeled garbage bins down.

The back door pushed open and the young girl exited with a bag of trash in each hand. She placed one on the ground and opened the top of garbage bin. She was throwing the second bag in when Kat approached.

"You okay?"

The girl spun with small cry, the top of the bin dropping with a crash.

Kat held up her hands. "Hey, hey. It's okay. It's just me. You served us tonight. Remember me?"

"He-hello?"

"Hi." Kat cleared her throat. "Are you okay?"

"I okay, yes. You scare me."

"Sorry about that." She reached for the girls arm. "I meant the bruises."

The girl pulled back and crossed her arms, hiding her wrists. "I am okay. Please leave." She backed toward the door. "Please."

"Look, I know you're frightened. I work at the detective agency across the from the convenience store a couple of blocks that way," she pointed. "If you need our help I'll do it for free. You don't have to pay, okay?"

The girl pulled open the back door and with one last glance at Kat entered and closed the door behind her.

"Well, that went as well as expected. Shit."

Chapter Six

"So what do we know?" Dan sat on the corner of the conference room table. Kat had her head buried in her laptop and Terry was leaning back in his chair, unshaven and looking very tired. A blue light flashed on the end of the thumb drive stuck in the side of his laptop. It was 10 a.m. They all looked like they'd been up all night.

Dan sipped cold coffee from a half-full large mug. "Anything? Anybody?"

Kat didn't lift her head from her screen. "Where's Beryl?"

"Hospital. You finding anything?"

She looked at him over the laptop lid. "I can piece together Andy's movements, sort of, from the locations on his phone. There aren't many, though. And intermittent. Give me a bit more time, okay?"

Dan didn't answer. Terry's chin was on his chest and he tried to stifle a yawn. "What about you?"

Terry surrendered to the yawn. "Sorry about that." He sniffed. "Video from the shops outside is transferring now." He pointed at his laptop. "I'll put it up on the wall in a sec." He tapped a key to wake the screen. "What have you done? And where the hell is Stew?"

"I still haven't heard from him. I've been calling around, hitting contacts, places Andy might hang out." He shook his head. "Not a lot of luck. He was seen at a chicken place in Wollongong a couple of days ago. Picked up a half chook and a small coleslaw. Bottle of water. Sat at an outside table, ate and left. Not that useful."

"If Stew was here he'd track him down."

"Well he fucking isn't, is he, Ter? You got that video yet?"

"Calm down, boys. We're all working together on this. Stew will get here when he gets here."

"Where the fuck did he go?"

Dan slid off the table and sat in his chair. "You're not his mum, Terry." He nodded at the large TV bolted to the wall. "Show me what you've got."

Terry mirrored his laptop to the wall display and opened a video. "No audio with this. It's from the backdoor from the restaurant next door."

"Put ours up. We've got audio."

Terry held his hand up. "Hang on. You'll see ours in a minute."

The video clip started. The camera faced the parking lot. The timestamp on the image showed that it was 5:47 the previous morning. The lot was empty and still in the early morning shadows. A dark blue Holden ute tore into the lot with a body rolling around the back.

"Is that Andy?" asked Kat.

"Yeah. Watch."

The truck juddered to a stop, Andy sliding up the bed, slamming against the wall separating the back from the cab. He moved slightly as the passenger-side door opened and a tall, wiry man stepped out. He was bald, and sinewy. He wore a dirty singlet and denims. Tattoos on both shoulders and down his left arm. He leaned into the back of the ute and grabbed Andy by the belt at the back of his trousers.

"Pause it." Dan leaned forward. "That guy — he's got to be almost 2 metres tall."

"And ugly as shit." Terry tapped the keyboard and continued the clip.

"Grab the best facial shot you can get when we're done."

"You bet."

On the clip the tall man lifted Andy out of the back of the ute by his belt, as easy as if he was lifting a sack of potatoes, and dropped him unceremoniously on the asphalt. He gave Andy a kick in the ribs and got back in the truck. It tore out of the lot.

"Pause and back it up. We get a rego number?"

Terry scrubbed the video back until the arse-end of the ute was clearest.

Kat scribbled a note. "Got it. I'll see what I can find."

"Now to *our* video."

Terry queued up a second video and started it. The rumble of the ute disappearing in the distance faded and Andy's groans got louder as he crawled into frame. The camera angled from above the backdoor, focussing on the entry, not the parking lot.

Andy pulled himself to his feet with one arm, the other wrapped around his ribs. *"Fucking hell."* He steadied himself against the doorframe and looked up at the camera. His face was bruised and bloody. He had a black eye and blood crusted above one eyebrow. He closed his eyes, took a shallow breath, winced and punched the code. 5-3-2-1-1. The 'click' of the latch releasing on the door was followed by Andy's groan as he pushed the door open and fell inside.

Terry stopped the video. "That's it. Blood stains up the stairs tell the rest of the story."

"Not much of a story," said Kat.

"Get that face back up on the screen."

Terry reopened the parking lot video and scrubbed to the point the tall passenger got out of the ute. He slowed it down until the face pointed most toward the camera. He froze the video and took a grab of his head, then zoomed it to fill the screen.

He had a hard look about him. He had day old stubble on his face and scalp. He had a chain tattooed around his neck and a devil on one of his shoulders.

Dan walked to the monitor. "Any of you recognise this guy?"

Terry and Kat joined him.

"He's not familiar, boss. Not a guy I'd forget. Not a guy I'd want to meet without a bunch of friends with me."

"Send copies to all of our phones." He sat back in his chair. "So what do we know?"

Kat slid in behind her laptop and unlocked the screen. There was a police report on the monitor. "The ute was stolen two days ago. Dead end there."

"How did they know where to dump Andy?"

Dan nodded. "I was thinking the same. He had to have run into them before the beating. We canvass with the photo."

Terry typed a couple of commands and his, Kat's and Dan's phones vibrated. "Picture sent."

"You've been quiet, Kat. You okay?"

She finger-combed her hair back and took a breath. "That guy was hardcore. I know I've only been here six months or so, but I've never heard of Andy getting smashed that hard. It doesn't happen, right? Maybe we should let the cops handle this one."

Dan was shaking his head before she finished talking. "No." He jabbed a finger in the direction of the screen with the bald guy's face still on it. "That guy is mine."

"Ours." Terry looked at Dan, then Kat. "All of ours."

"We've just got to find him."

Kat crossed her arms. "Him? There are many 'hims'." She pointed at the face on the screen. "And if I've learned anything working here, that guy is pretty low on the totem pole if he's doing the dumping. There's an organisation of guys like that doing something they don't want us knowing about. This is bigger than the three of us. We really should be letting the police handle this. You know that Warren Peters guy pretty well, right? That cop? We should give him this photo, and the video, and - and the locations I've found from Andy's phone, and the rego from the truck. They've got way more resources — and firepower — than we do."

Terry leaned forward, finger pointed at Kat. Dan pulled him back. "You're assuming we're rational, Kat. We're not going to get in the way of whatever the police do." He nodded at the screen. "You're right about that guy. He's a cog. The cops find him and maybe a couple of his associates and they'll consider it a job well done. And we'll help the cops — help us. I want to wrap up the whole organisation. And you're right about that, too." He sat back. "We're going to need help."

Kat closed her laptop with a little more force than necessary. "Great. Go find some help. I'm going to stop by the hospital and see how Andy is doing."

Dan waited until she left the room before he spoke again. "This is going to get rough, Terry. You okay with that?"

Terry closed his laptop, a little more gently. "I kinda agree with Kat. This is a police job. But I get what you say. They'll get done what needs to get done to resolve Andy's beating. But they won't go deeper unless something obvious drops on their desks." He swallowed. "And we need to go deeper." He nodded. "I'm in. Who are you going to get to help us? And where the fuck is Stew?"

Chapter Seven

Kat leaned on the counter at the nurses station waiting for the young guy at reception to get off the phone. He read something off the monitor to whoever was on the other end of the call, then hung up and smiled at Kat.

"Sorry about that. What can I do for you?"

Kat looked at his name tag. "Tim, I'm here to see Andy Smith. Which room is he in?"

"Are you family?"

"I may as well be. The only family I know about are his parents and they're in WA and we can't reach them. I work with him. He came in pretty bashed up yesterday. I just want to make sure he's okay."

Tim looked at her for a beat, then opened a screen on his workstation. "Andrew Smith?"

"Andy. He was in surgery last night. One of our other colleagues should be here also." She took a breath and smiled. "Andy. He doesn't like Andrew. Or Smithee."

Tim nodded. "He's in bed 12B. Room 12 just down the hall, bed closest to the window."

"Thank you so much. How is he?"

"Confidentiality laws forbid me from telling you," said Tim with a smile. "Ask him yourself."

Kat tapped on the counter. "Great. Thanks heaps." She walked down the hall and stood in the doorway of room 12. A privacy curtain split the room half way in and spanned three-quarters of the width of the room. A comfortable looking chair was angled in the corner. Beryl's purse sat on the chair.

She eased her head around the edge of the curtain. Beryl was sitting in a second chair, reading. Andy was unconscious, an IV bag dripping stuff into one arm and half a dozen sensors recording vitals on multiple screens.

"How's he doing?"

Beryl started and looked up from her book. She put a finger to her lips. "Ssshh. He needs his rest," she whispered.

Kat put Beryl's purse on the window ledge and pulled the other chair close. "I thought he was okay."

"He'll live, but he was beat up pretty bad. Healing is exhausting."

"Have you talked to him? What happened?"

"He's only been awake for a few minutes. Didn't say anything about what happened. Mentioned someone named Kelly, or Kelly-Anne. Then he faded again."

Kat thought for a second. "I don't know anyone named Kelly. Do you?"

Beryl shook her head. "Not in this context. It's no doubt the 'her' he was talking about when he said to 'find her'." She scratched her nose. "It's going to be many hours before he's conscious again. There's no point in you staying here."

"You've been here since dawn, almost, I think. I'll take a shift."

"I still have a half a book to finish and there's no way I can do that in the office with a clear conscience. And if I'm there, I can't be here, and I really need to be here. He needs to see a familiar face when he wakes up."

Kat raised an eyebrow and pointed at herself. "Face. Kinda familiar."

"Not as familiar as mine. Has anybody reached his parents yet?"

"No. We'll keep trying." Kat surrendered to the inevitable. "Call me as soon as he wakes up. There's almost no evidence helping us figure out what happened."

Beryl scowled. "Tell Dan to work whatever he's got. We're not waiting until Andy wakes up to start this."

"We're working it." She held up her phone and showed her the headshot of the guy who dropped Andy off. "This guy, and some friends, deposited Andy at the back door."

Beryl held up her phone. "Terry sent it to me, too. Head back to the office and find the son of a bitch."

"Fine. Call me if he says anything."

She tapped on the nurse's counter on the way out. "Thanks, Timmy."

"Beryl kicked you out?"

"She wants to stay."

"She is what I wish my mother had been."

Kat nodded. "You and me both. Catch you later."

Kat punched the code at the back door and took the stairs two at a time. "Dan."

The place was empty. "Terry? Dan?" She stuck in her head in the conference room. "Jesus. The place is wide open. Come on in. Steal our shit."

The front door opened and feet clomped up the stairs. Kat ducked into the conference room and held her breath. She heard a clink of someone taking a glass out of the kitchen cupboard and the water running, filling up the glass.

A long drink, followed by a sigh and Stew saying, "Where in the hell is everybody?"

Kat let out her breath and stepped out of the conference room and into the kitchen. "Where in the hell were *you*?" She stopped short when she saw him. "Are you okay?"

Stew's left eye was swollen almost shut and his lower lip was split. His handlebar moustache was stained with blood, and a smear of dried blood streaked across the side of his neck, like he missed it when wiping off other blood. The knuckles on both hands were bruised and raw.

"I'm fine. Where's Dan? We need to talk."

"I'm assuming he and Terry are looking for the guy who did that to you. I just got back from the hospital and this place was empty."

Stew pointed at his face. "Yeah. I've run into him. The photo Terry sent, right? Yeah. Him and this bird who is just as vicious as he is. More. Dan and Terry better hope they don't run into them. She's a particular kind of insane." He took another drink, wincing as the glass touched his split lip. "How's Andy?"

"Recovering post-surgery. Beryl's with him."

He nodded and rubbed the back of his head. "When are Dan and Terry back?"

Kat typed a message on her phone. "Right now would be good. You need to tell us what you know. 'Cause we know pretty much fuck all."

Her phone chimed. "They're a couple minutes out. You should sit. You look like shit."

"I feel like shit. I'm getting old." He grabbed a mug out of the cupboard and talk was suspended while the coffee machine ground beans. He sat with the cup of black coffee, took a sip and sighed. "This is a weird one."

"Thirty-six hours, almost. Where were you?" Kat held up her hand. "No, wait for the others."

The door to the office opened and Dan called out. "Stew. Where the hell are you?"

"Kitchen."

Dan poked his head in. "Meeting room." He kept walking.

Stew groaned as he stood. "Fuuuck, I hurt." He took his coffee with him.

Terry opened his laptop and mirrored it to the wall display. He put up the picture of the guy from the truck. He waited until everyone sat. "This guy," he said and turned to Stew. "Have you - oh shit, what happened to your face?"

He jabbed his finger toward the monitor. "*That* guy happened to my face. And his girlfriend."

Terry looked at Dan, then back to Stew. "Only two people? And one of them was a - "

"Shut your mouth, Terry," said Kat. "You don't think a girl can hit hard? Come here. I'll show you."

"Yeah, sorry, not what I meant. This is *Stew* we're talking about. Cleaning up two thugs is all in a day's work."

"Right."

Dan knocked on the table to bring things to order. "Stew, this guy dropped Andy off at the back door. We haven't heard anything from Andy yet, so all we've got is whatever we have in this room. You've met this guy, I take it."

"This guy is named Jason, and the woman he works with is, if I heard right, Rhonda. We've got a fight on our hands, Dan."

Dan nodded. "We haven't had much luck. This pic from the restaurant's security feed, the rego of the truck they were driving, which was stolen a couple of days prior, and a few, intermittent locations from Andy's phone. What did you dig up?"

"What locations?"

"Doesn't matter. I've only been able to dig out half a dozen. Speckled around the area." Kat opened her laptop and unlocked it. "Where did you run into, what's his name, Jason?"

"The locations, Kat. Andy turned off geolocations on his phone almost six months ago. If there are any locations showing up at all it's because he turned them on. What were they?"

Kat read through a list. "Port Kembla. That's south of Wollongong. A place in Airds, like maybe five minutes from here, the restaurant we went to last night, then a farm in northwest Sydney and a place on the Central Coast." She cocked her head. "So, we're just going to go visit these places and ask them why Andy was there?"

"Not until we've talked to Andy," said Dan. "How's he doing?"

"Still out. At least he was when I left. Beryl is mother-henning him." Kat closed her laptop. "Enough from us. What hit your face?"

Stew scratched at the stubble on his cheek. "Where to start?"

Dan smiled. "The usual place."

"Right. The beginning. First of all, I'm kinda pissed off that Andy didn't come to me. If he was looking for someone, he shoulda come to me. I'm the person who can find anyone. He wouldn't be in the hospital if he came to me." Stew cleared his throat. "Be that as it may."

He took out his phone and opened the message Terry had sent. "I got the photo after this guy beat on me. With his girlfriend. So, better late than never, I guess." He flipped the phone over.

"I talked to the locals, got the truck's rego. It was stolen, as you already know, but that didn't make it invisible. I tracked it down, found them at a servo in Airds. They filled and ran without paying. I followed them, but they caught my tail. Led me to an out of the way place and cleaned my clock."

"That's the part that interests me."

Stew shook his head. "I think maybe I was put off balance by the woman half of the team. She looked sturdy, but, first, I've never felt a woman hit that hard before and second, I'm not comfortable hitting a woman. I wasn't. I am now. Under certain circumstances."

"So there was a fight, but they left you alive. They left you in better shape than Andy. How'd that happen?"

"I got my licks in, Dan. I'm not completely useless. When I left them, Jason was flat on his back and Rhonda, if that's her name, was a bit loopy. It was a lucky shot. I pissed off while I could. I wouldn't have survived another round with the two of them."

"Any hint about what Andy was up to?"

"I asked. They were not forthcoming." He rubbed his jaw. "Andy was a fucking ghost. I have no idea what he was looking into, what he found, or why those two had such massive hard-ons for him."

"So we're back to square one. We've got zero." said Terry.

"Not quite." Kat patted her laptop. "We know the places he visited. They're significant, according to Stew. So not zero."

"No. Just half a bee's dick more than zero."

Chapter Eight

The Fern Tree was an innocuous building sitting on the hill overlooking Newport Beach and Newport Marina on the Northern Beaches, some 40 km north of Sydney proper. There was no signage other than the A4-sized brass plaque on the outside wall beside the door. Someone walking down the street wouldn't be able tell it was one of the oldest, most exclusive gentlemen's club in Sydney. And if they didn't have an invitation and $45,000 a year membership dues, they'd never see the inside.

Heavy drapes worked with the thick carpet to cancel any echoes. Wall mounted lights provided enough illumination to be comfortable. It was like the inside of a dark, rich German chocolate cake.

Samuel Prescott had been a member for twenty-seven years. It was a present to himself on his thirtieth birthday. This was his home away from home. That it was adjacent to a marina was irrelevant. He hated boats and the opulence they advertised. He preferred anonymity. Only a very select few knew what he did. The assumption, one he fostered, was old money combined with smart real estate investments. The latter part wasn't that far off. But the money wasn't old. Far from it.

He refreshed his drink and sat in the chair at the side of a large hearth. Ironbark logs sat in a two metre wide grate. It was too warm outside to light it now, but in July it roared, the ambience belying the non-socially acceptable deals he set up.

He checked the time. The meet, the presentation of the catalogue, started in thirty minutes. A few of his clients were known to show up early, in hopes of getting a jump on the game, and were always disappointed. He had good product, had the utmost discretion and essentially a money back guarantee.

He rested his hand on the catalogue. Always hardcopies, never anything overtly descriptive online. Each item had a lot number referenced in any electronic communications. Twenty-two items. Prices on fifteen, starting at $15,000 each and moving up in line with the rarity of the commodity to $75,000. The last seven were so exquisite, so rare, that they were only available by auction.

That was for another day, though. Tonight was whetting the appetite, setting the reserve for the auctions, aligning the product in the buyers' eyes with the assigned lot numbers. The real show had the actual merchandise on display and was scheduled for a few days hence.

He took another sip of whiskey and almost choked on it. Jason and Rhonda had just walked into the room, not looking their best.

Jason stood almost a head taller than Samuel. He wore denim jeans and a tight ash-blue T-shirt. A size too small by the looks of it. He wasn't bulky, but he was big. He had a swimmer's physique, narrow at the waist and increasingly larger as you went up. His shoulders were like bowling balls. His head was recently shaved. He had a deep purple bruise under his left eye and a bandage on his left ear.

Rhonda was shorter, but no less tough looking. Her skin was tanned and her hair cut short. Her arms were lean and sinewy. Her fists were clenched and jaw set. She had a slight limp and a bruise on her jaw.

Samuel looked around quickly. "What in the *hell* are you doing here?" he spat. "By my invitation only. And tonight is definitely NOT the night. How in the hell did you get in here dressed like that?"

"I convinced them," said Rhonda. They sat either side of him.

Jason slid his hand along the burled walnut arm of the chair he was sitting in. "Nice place, Sammy. You should invite us here more often. Wouldn't have to crash the joint."

"Why are you here?"

"We, Rho and I, had another run-in."

"I thought you put that guy in the hospital."

Rhonda stretched her legs and winced. "We did. Different guy. Same outfit, I gather. This guy was tougher."

Samuel's foot bounced. He took a furtive glance at his watch and cleared his throat. "So you put him in the hospital, too?"

"That's the thing, boss." Rhonda picked at a cuticle. "He got the better of us. This is a heads up that he's probably going to try working his way up the chain to get to you."

Samuel leaned forward. "What do you mean? What did you say to him? He knows my name?"

"Fuck no," said Jason. "These guys aren't chumps, though. We're going to close them down, but it might take a couple of days. In that time, they might uncover some shit."

Samuel held up his finger and shook his head. "No. No fucking way. You two stay out of it. You're too close to me." He snapped his fingers. "Those two Russkies — Vasily and Ilya. What are they doing right now?"

"Waiting for the shipment. Trying to stay out of trouble, I hope."

"Give it to them. Get them the details and stay out of their way. And make sure they know I want nothing left of whoever it is scratching at my door." He took a breath. A decision had been made. "Now get the fuck out of here before my customers arrive."

"Not even going to buy us a drink?" Rhonda smiled and stood. "If you see the Russians before we do, tell them to call me."

Samuel watched them walk out, slower than he would have liked. He closed his eyes for a second, then typed a message into his phone and pressed send.

"Fuck." He downed his drink and poured another two fingers from a decanter. "Son of a fuck." He rested his fingertips on the folder. At least a million in there. Easily a million. Double if the buyers got caught in the heat of the moment. He'd had a smooth run over the past couple of decades. Five or six consignments a year, roughly a million apiece and never a sniff of trouble. He had enough to quit and live comfortably. Very comfortably. A small smile played across his face. But where would the fun be in that?

Gene Hobson, tall, thin and as always with a slight pallor, came in, looked around, then sat beside him and touched the portfolio. He raised his eyebrows. "May I?"

Samuel lifted his hand. "Absolutely. That's why we're here."

Gene opened the folder and immediately went to the pages at the back.

Samuel nodded to himself. Gene always went for the high end. "Once we've all gathered, we'll be setting the reserve for those products. Only lot numbers will be referenced, so remember which ones you like."

Gene brushed his fingertips over the page. "Exquisite. Beautiful condition. Pristine?"

"Pristine."

"Arrival?"

"The next couple of days. Details will be shared on the usual board. You're interested?"

"Always." He grinned, crooked teeth filling his mouth. He pressed his index finger on the picture. "Mine."

"You know how it goes, Gene. No pre-sales for the auctioned pieces. And a thirty percent premium for pre-sale on those with prices. The product with prices go first. The auctions are at the end of the sale, and you have as much of a chance as any." Samuel cleared his throat and sat back. "Getting here early only hurts you, I think. You find a favourite, convince yourself it's yours, and end up bidding more than you intended to." He held up his hands. "Not that I'm complaining. It's appreciated."

Gene nodded in thought. "Who else is showing up?"

"Tonight or the day of the sale?"

"Both. Is Adam showing up tonight?"

Samuel nodded. "He said he was going to be a few minutes late. Chris will be here, Mark, Louise - "

"She is?"

"Yeah. Why not? Her money is a good as yours."

"I don't know." Gene rubbed the palms of his hands on his thighs. "I don't trust her."

Samuel sighed. "Security is top notch. She's trustworthy. She's in this just as deep as you are."

Gene scratched the back of his head as another man came in, short, stout and sweaty, and sat in a chair on the other side of Samuel.

"Laurence."

"Sammy. How ya doing?"

"Haven't seen you in over a year. Where have you been?" Samuel clenched his jaw muscles. "Everything okay?"

"Schmick." He looked around. "Adam going to be here?"

"He said he would."

"Good. He owes me some money." He took the folder from Gene and flipped to the front. He slowly poured over the pictures. "Good quality product. As usual." He lingered over one. "I couldn't persuade you to reserve this one for me, could I?"

Samuel smiled and took the folder back. "Thirty percent premium to buy one of the listed items ahead of time."

"Is that a new thing? It should be at a discount. I give you money ahead of time."

"You're trying to jump the queue. That brings a service charge. And maybe we should wait until the others arrive and discuss this then."

"And drive up demand? Why not auction all of them?"

Samuel sat back, interlaced his fingers on his lap and smiled. "Sounds like a good idea." He looked at the other early arrivals. "Agreed?"

"Laurence can fuck right off. We're not auctioning the full lot." Gene wiped spittle from the corners of his mouth. "Not even sure why he's invited."

"He's invited because I invited him. You're right, though. Standard process. Fifteen with prices and when they're dispersed, we auction the exquisitely rare pieces."

"You're going to have to tell me one day how you get them into the country. Packed in a crate of coffee to avoid the sniffer dogs?" Gene laughed.

"No, I don't have to tell you and if you bring it up again I'm uninviting you. And then I'll have you shot." Prescott smiled, but nobody was absolutely certain if he was joking.

Three more cookie-cutter middle-aged, affluent white men and a short, thin woman with close-cropped black hair strolled in together.

"We doing this?" asked Louise. "Where's the book?"

Gene took it from Laurence and handed it to her. "The, um," he cleared his throat. "Item number seven looks good."

Samuel looked at his watch. "Okay, five more minutes and we move to the private room and get started."

Nathan watched from a large comfortable chair across the room as the last person left. Laurence, he thought. An odious person, but a reliable payer. His boss left the private room last and sat beside him. He passed Nathan a handful of paper chits. He butted the edges together and quickly checked the amounts.

"More than usual."

"Weird thing, today. I told them there was a 30% premium if they wanted to buy a non-auction piece tonight, before the show. Seemed to drive demand. Some eager buyers this tranche."

Nathan fanned the papers. Each contained a name, a dollar figure and bank details. He did some quick mental math. "Over eight hundred thousand. Not a bad haul for a pre-sale, without looking at the actual product."

Samuel took a deep breath and smiled. "That's thirteen of the twenty-two. Put it in the escrow account. Two more will go at a flat rate on the night. One priced at thirty-five thou and one at fifty. The other seven are auction only. This is going to come in at well over one point five mill. Maybe pushing two." He laughed at the look on Nathan's face. "I want you on hand for the auction." He slapped both hands down on the chair arms. "I need to touch base with Jen. I'm not happy with the delay. The logistics need to be fixed."

Nathan looked at his watch. "She should be in the coffee shop across the street. You can catch her there."

Samuel shook his head. "Send the car around and tell her to join me." He stood and made his way to the entrance. A Mercedes stopped and the driver hopped out and opened the back door. Samuel looked over the roof at the coffee shop and watched Nathan talk to Jenny.

Jen was middle-aged and severe. Her face was angular and her greying hair pulled back in a tight ponytail. Her skirt fell below her knees and she wore a cardigan over her plain blouse, even in the heat of the day. She nodded at Nathan, collected her purse and walked across the street and got in the back seat with Samuel.

He waited until the door was closed and the car moving. "Jen. I trust you're well."

"Well enough," said Jen. "What's wrong?"

"I was about to ask the same. Why has the shipment been delayed?" He held up his hand. "The root cause, Jen. Not the fact that we didn't have a man at the port. *Why* didn't we have a man at the port? And then three more whys deeper. The story about the shift change is thin. What can we do to ensure that unfortunate problem doesn't happen again?"

Jenny stammered. "I - I - I'm sure it won't. Positive."

He looked at his watch. "You've got forty-five minutes to convince me of that. You need to tell me where the gap was, why that gap occurred, and what you, as head of my logistics, are going to do to ensure that gap no longer exists."

"It was - unexpected. Our man at the port was out of place. He had an emergency of some sort at home and swapped shifts. At exactly the time we needed him at the port."

"And no contingencies in place." A tight smile flitted across his face. "Unfortunate."

Jenny straightened the pleats in her skirt. "I've — we've — been following these procedures for over a decade with no problems."

"Perhaps becoming complacent." He thought for a second. "Take this opportunity to review the process from beginning to end. From collection and departure overseas, how the product is smuggled out of the source countries and how we smuggle into Australia. Is Port Kembla still the best place? Should we move it to Newcastle? Do we transfer immediately at docking, or leave the product unattended but contained and recover later? Look at all of it. The next shipment after this one is two months out. I want new plans within a month."

Chapter Nine

Vasily was meth-sinewy, though he never used the drug. He had three days of stubble on his head and five on his face. He wore a Mötley Crüe T-shirt and baggy jeans with a zoo map in his back pocket. At less than 170 cm, he looked like that last person you'd expect to see if someone told you a Russian enforcer was going to show up.

He was watching penguins at Taronga Zoo with Ilya, the kind of person you *would* expect to see if someone told you a Russian enforcer was going to show up. He had a thick layer of fat covering slabs of muscle on his 1900 cm frame. Pale, almost white, blue eyes, a little closer together than average, peered through thick brows over a repeatedly busted, never set quite right, nose.

"Cute birdies," said Ilya.

Vasily looked up from his phone. "What? Yeah. Cute. Fucking things cannot fly, though, so they are pretty useless as birds."

"They fly in the water, man."

Vasily looked up at him for a second. "That is swimming, stupid." He held up his phone. "We got something to do." He handed the phone over.

Ilya squinted and held the phone close to his face. "Where is this place?"

"I do not know. I have not looked yet." He took the phone back. "This guy, he bested Jase and Rho."

"That is a word? 'Bested'? It does not sound right."

Vasily stuck the address in his GPS. "Fucking hell."

Ilya looked over his shoulder. "An hour? Jesus."

"Yeah. But we are getting food first. And I want to see the bird show at the amphe—ampithe—that stage thing at the far end of the zoo. We go later."

"That message seems very urgent."

"Sometime today will be good enough. As long as we finish before when the cargo arrives. We have to go south for the cargo anyway. Maybe this is a good thing. Whoa." Vasily nudged his large partner. "Look."

A family of four -- mum, dad and twin girls just hitting puberty -- walked past. The father looked like a middle-management accountant in cargo pants, golf shirt and socks and sandals. He had his face permanently stuck in a hobby digital SLR camera with a long lens and, more likely than not, a permanent place in his closet in about a month. Mum was in shorts and a blouse, hair up in a ponytail, purse over her shoulder and a bored look on her face that screamed wine, and now, and lots of it.

The two girls were what caught Vasily's attention. They had just entered puberty and had the awkwardness of a colt. Long legs to short shorts, bare midriffs and small T-shirts, topped with smiling faces and long, curly brown hair.

"Twins. Damn."

Ilya scowled. "Not the time or place, *mate*. We have job to do."

"Okay, okay. We look only. We follow."

"And get arrested, following."

"No. We are also tourists. We just happen to walk the same direction those two perfect asses are walking." He watched the girls walk. "Those asses, right?"

Ilya grunted. "Too young for me. I like my women with experience, and padding. Not bony little babies."

Vasily smiled. "You can watch, then."

The family stopped in front of the giraffe enclosure. The two girls walked up the steps to a platform that put them eye-to-eye with a young calf. One of the girls had a fist full of grass. She held it out and the giraffe's tongue wrapped around her hand retrieving its snack.

She let out a squeal and a giggle and wiped her hand on her shorts. "Gross. Giraffe snot."

Vasily smiled and hung back. The girls fed the giraffe a couple more times, then bounced down the steps.

"Capybaras next, daddy," squealed one of them.

Vasily checked the map and nudged Ilya. "This way."

"You are on your own. I will get some food." Ilya shook his head and wandered away, following his nose.

Vasily got to the capybara enclosure before the family. He held back until they leaned against the railing. Mum was on the left, the two girls then dad on the right. He licked his lips and stepped up behind the girls. He took out his mobile and started taking pictures, leaning forward and pressing against one of the teens.

She squirmed, pushed back and called out to her father. "Daddy. This man is touching me."

It was mum who responded first, though. She reached over and pushed Vasily. "Creep. John, this man was violating Lizzie."

Vasily stumbled back, laughing, with his hands up. "No, no. You are making mistake." He pointed at his mobile. "I was just taking pictures of giant rats. I didn't even see this little girl."

Dad sucker punched him, knocking him on his arse, surprising both dad and Vasily. He shook out his hand and took a step back. "You get the fuck out of here, creep, before I do that again."

Vasily chuckled as he stood, brushing dust off his trousers. "I let you have that one, pops, but you do not do that again if you want to go home and not the hospital."

"Daddy, I felt his thing pressed against me."

Mum shoved him from behind again. He spun, hand reaching for the knife in his back pocket. He checked himself. A crowd was forming. Security was moving in from the outside edge.

"You are all mistaken. I thought Australia was friendly place. I am mistaken." He glanced at the oncoming security, smiled at the teens and licked his lips and turned to walk away.

"You son of a bitch." Mum jumped on his back and wrapped an arm around his neck. She yanked backward, pulling them both onto the ground, her on the bottom, Vasily on his back on top of her. Her right arm was around his neck, her legs wrapped around his waist and she was punching his ear with her left hand.

Vasily roared and tried rolling over to get purchase on the ground. Dad and two security men got there first and pulled them apart.

Vasily struggled free of the two security guards. "Let me go. I am leaving now." He saw Ilya approaching from behind the security guards, his face menacing, and gently shook his head. "My mistake. Sensitive woman. American, right? I should have known. I go now."

He walked backward for a few steps then turned and started walking quickly to the exit, a smile on his face. The security followed. Ilya caught up with him and fell into step beside him.

"You are fucking stupid, Vas. You get arrested and you are on your own."

"It was worth it." He took out his phone. "We need to get to work anyway. There is this guy in Campbelltown." He looked at Ilya. "You in for a fight?"

Ilya rolled his shoulders. "Always."

"Good. Now we go to this Campbelltown place." He held up a photo on his phone. "This guy beat boss's two best."

Ilya's eyes narrowed. "If they are the best, and they lost to this guy, what does the boss think we can do?"

"We know. They did not. And he does not know we are coming. We watch for a little while then remove him when he is not expecting us, no?"

Ilya got in the driver's seat of their rental Toyota. "Give me the address." He started the car and typed the address into the onboard GPS. "An hour and three minutes." He sighed. "This country is too fucking big."

Vasily smacked him on the arm with the back of his hand. "We are from fucking Russia. Big. Bullshits."

"Right. You Google about this place we are going to while I drive."

Dan crossed the street and caught up to Terry who handed him a thumb drive. "What did you get, Ter?"

"Video from a couple of shops. Don't show us anything we don't already have. This is a waste of time. We need to check those locations Andy visited. I know, they're all over the place, but we have to, and we have to soon."

Dan nodded. "I need to find out what Warren knows. Stew is on his way to the Central Coast. He knows a guy up there who may help. Get the address in Port Kembla from Kat and head down there and ask around. See what you can find out. When I'm finished with Wazza I'll check another address. Keep in touch, okay? Nothing fancy, just look."

"Don't worry, boss. I'm not going to get myself in a fight."

Stew parked his car across the street from The Pelican, a family owned cafe on the Central Coast. He turned off the engine and sat in thought for a second. He wasn't sure what his reception would be. He was currently dating the ex-wife of the man he was about to meet. Mac Durridge was a Private Investigator and ex-cop and Stew found it difficult to read the man.

He sighed and pushed himself out of the car. No point putting it off any longer.

He pulled open the front door, transitioning from hot summer sun into the air conditioned cool and muted sounds of the cafe.

A young blonde woman in shorts, T-shirt and a high ponytail smiled at him and grabbed a menu. "Hi there. I'm Jessie. Table for one?"

Stew looked past her into the gloom. "I'm meeting someone here. Mac-"

"Durridge?" She put the menu back in the pile. "He's in the back." Her ponytail flicked as she turned away. "He's in a mood."

Stew took a deep breath and found Mac in a booth, nursing a cup of coffee in the half dark. "Mac? Stew. I called."

A half smile cracked Mac's face. "You're the man." He jabbed a finger in his direction. "You're the guy who locked down Jane. I am eternally grateful to you."

Stew slid into the booth across from him. "I'm the guy? Was expecting a different response, if I'm honest."

Mac sipped his coffee and smiled. He put the cup down and knocked his spoon to the floor. He winced with the clatter. "Feeling a bit rough. I'm delighted Jane won't be coming after me for support payments anymore." He grunted as he leaned over his pot belly to pick up the spoon.

"Right." Stew laced his fingers and rested his hands on the table. "She told me that was done a couple of years ago. Some weenie named Tony."

Mac acknowledged that with a smile and raised eyebrows. "Ya got me. I enjoy complaining. Give me more details about why you're up here and what you want me to do."

Stew opened the photos on his phone and scrolled to Jason's picture. He placed the phone on the table and slid it toward Mac. "Looking for this guy. He and a partner beat the shit out of one of our guys."

Mac glanced and slide it slightly away from him. "Big whoop. I get beat up all the time. It's a perk of the business, wouldn't you say?"

Stew picked up the phone. "He beat up Andy. Andy never gets beat. Not unless there's half a dozen or more. He'd gone quiet for a few days, working on something he didn't tell us about. His phone pinged in a couple of places. One of them was up here. Hoping you could lend a hand looking around for us. We're running pretty thin on the ground."

"My rates - "

"Whatever the fuck they are, we'll pay it."

Mac sat back and pursed his lips. "My hangover seems to have dissipated a bit. I'll see what I can do. The pings — how do you know they're relevant?"

Stew pulled his phone back. "He turned location services around six months ago. If something registered, it was intentional."

"Where up here?"

"Wamberal area. I'll send you the coordinates." He typed a command in his phone. "Should be in your inbox."

Mac nodded. "Rules of engagement?"

"Recce for the minute. I don't want them to know they are under surveillance. Do some discrete sniffing around and see if this guy rings any bells. See if you can find out what he's up to." He paused. "But don't let him find you or you'll end up smashed."

"Andy called me almost a week ago. Told me he'd be up this way and would contact me when he was in town." Mac shook his head. "Didn't hear from him again."

Chapter Ten

Kat looked out the passenger window of Dan's car. They were a few minutes away from the location Andy had pinged in Airds. "Are you kidding me?"

"What?"

"That's a juvenile detention centre, and it shares a fence with a public school."

Dan leaned down and looked through the passenger window. "Yup. Lads under fifteen years old. Broken homes. Runaways caught up with older arseholes. Some of them dropped out of the high school across the street. Some of them didn't even get there."

"Oh my God. You're a softy."

He shrugged. "Just missed out on that path myself. I was good at sports, otherwise…"

She sat in silence. She glanced at him and back out at the detention centre.

Dan checked the map on his dashboard, turned right and rolled to a stop in front of a two storey double brick house. The lawn was overgrown. Curtains were drawn and the house looked empty. Dan put the car in park. "This place. Andy blipped here. Something in this house. Maybe someone."

Kat nodded. "Now what?"

"We walk. Both sides of the street. Door knock and see if anyone knows the man who thrashed Andy."

"Seems a bit dangerous if we find him."

"We'll work together. A missing persons investigation. We're on our turf and if we bump into him, hey, we found him."

Kat laughed. "Okay, boss."

His phone rang as he pushed open the car door. "McGinnis."

"Dan, it's me," said Beryl. "How fast can you get to the hospital?"

He got back in the car and closed the door. "Andy ok?" He motioned for Kat to get back in. "We can be there in fifteen minutes."

"He's fine. He's waking up. The doctor says he's doing well. Time to get some questions answered."

"I'll call the others."

"I already did. Terry just got to the Gong and has turned around. He's half an hour out. Stew is a little farther. They'll come straight here."

"We're on our way." He hung up and tossed the phone in the centre console.

"Andy ok?" asked Kat.

"Waking up. Beryl says he's doing well. Hopefully he's got some answers. Might save us some time."

Kat looked at the house. "Yeah. And some bruises."

Beryl met them in a waiting room on the ground floor. "Any luck?" she asked.

"Finding the guy? No. Barely got started when you called. I think Kat's a little disappointed she didn't get to rough someone up."

Kat flexed a bicep. "Strewth." She winked at Beryl. "Andy's awake?"

"Being attended to by some nurses and that Doctor Jane Stew's all excited about."

"When can we get in to talk to him?"

"Let's head in now."

Jane was making a notation in Andy's chart when Beryl, Dan and Kat came in the room. Kat pulled back the curtain splitting the room and sat on the edge of the empty bed.

Andy's face was bruised, but that, and the fact that he was in the hospital, were the only signs he'd been on the receiving end of a battle.

"You alive?"

He smiled weakly and raised his hand to say hi. "I'll live. You all didn't have to come here. I'll be out in a couple of days."

Jane snorted. "Only if you're stupid." She glanced at the chart again. "Okay. Maybe a couple of days." She hung the chart on the end of his bed and walked out.

Andy tried to push himself up to a sitting position and groaned. "My fucking ribs. Everything else I could live with just fine, but my ribs are killing me."

"More morphine?" Kat's stood and reached for the dispensing mechanism.

"No, no. Makes my brain fuzzy. Where are the other two?"

"Trying to find out who did this to you," said Dan. "Smart move with the phone. Terry's in the Gong and Stew's on his way back from the Central Coast."

Andy winced and finished pushing himself upright. "Jesus. Terry will get pulled apart by those two."

Terry rapped on the doorframe and walked in. "Didn't lay a glove on me. Didn't even get there. What's at Port Kembla?"

Andy took a steadying breath. "Stay out of this one, guys. It's personal, not business."

"Bullshit." Beryl crossed her arms. "This makes it business."

And held his hands up. "No, no. I can't drag you all into this."

"You don't have a choice, mate," said Dan. "We're in it now whether you like it or not."

Jane entered and cleared her throat. "That's enough. Visiting hours are over. He needs to heal. Doesn't matter how tough he thinks he is, his body has a mind of its own."

Stew walked into the room behind her. "Cracking the whip

again?"

Jane spun. "Where in the hell were you?"

"Visiting one of your old flames. Mac says hi."

She stared at him for a second. "What were you doing up there?"

"He's going to help us out with a case." He took Jane by the shoulders and gently moved her out of the way. "Excuse me, Doctor. I've got a beef with your patient."

"Wait a second. Mac? Is he coming down here? I moved here to get away from that piece of shit."

"I doubt he'll be down here anytime soon." Stew stepped up to the bed and leaned close to Andy's face. He spoke in a low voice.

"What the fuck, over?"

Andy slid back to a lying position. "What?"

"So you were looking for someone. Took you all over the state and," he moved his hand around over Andy's prone form, "you got schooled on how to fight. Did you find whoever you were looking for?"

Andy shook his head. "No."

"No. Am I surprised? No. I'm not. Who in McGinnis Investigations is the go to guy when it comes to finding missing persons? Is it Beryl? No. Is it Terry? Fuck no. He couldn't find his nuts if they weren't in a bag."

"Hey."

He gripped the railing on the edge of the bed tight enough to whiten his knuckles. "Ten years. Ten motherfucking years you've known me. Ten years I've known you. And if you weren't flat out on your back right now in the hospital, I'd put you in here myself."

"Did you find her?"

"No. Because you didn't come to us for help finding her. Whoever 'her' is."

Jane pushed in beside him. "His blood pressure is rising. Time to take a break, guys. Give my patient some time to heal, okay?"

"We're not finished yet," barked Stew. He closed his eyes and took a deep breath. "Sorry, Jane. Give us a couple of minutes and we'll leave this guy in your capable hands."

Jane glared at Stew for a minute, glanced at her watch. "Two minutes."

He took her hand. "Thanks. And, again, sorry for barking. I'll make it up to you."

She pulled her hand away and tapped on her watch. "One minute, forty-five."

Stew nodded. "Okay. Andy, what was so importantly private you had to keep this to yourself?"

He shook his head and looked up at Stew. "It's my business."

Stew clenched his jaw and was about to bark back when Kat placed a hand on his arm. "Relax, Stew. He can't find her, whoever she is, in here, and he's not going to be in any shape to look for her for at least a couple of weeks after he gets out. He'll come around. The longer he takes, the dumber he is, the harder it will be to find her."

Andy grit his teeth and sat up, trying to reach for the top drawer in the small table beside his bed.

"Let me." Terry opened the drawer. Andy's personal effects — his wallet and watch — were in the drawer. "What are you looking for?"

"Wallet."

He took the worn, black leather wallet and handed it to Andy. "Gonna pay us off to leave you alone?"

He shook his head. "Showing you who I was looking for." He fished a photo out of one of the clear plastic pockets. The girl looked to be ten years old. Big brown eyes, straight black hair in a thick plait and honey-brown skin. She had a huge smile on her face with barely noticeable braces. He looked at the picture for a second then handed it to Stew. "Her. I need to find her."

Stew took the picture. "Cute kid." He handed the picture back to Andy. "Even more of a reason to have me involved. You are clearly shit house at finding people."

Andy carefully slid the photo back into his wallet. "I didn't want to involve the company, although it appears I don't have a choice in the matter now."

"Why not?" asked Beryl. "It's what we do."

"It's personal. She's my daughter, Kaliyanei. Kelly."

Chapter Eleven

There was dead silence in the hospital room, long enough for Andy to look at each of his friends' stunned faces.

Dan broke the silence. "What the fuck? Ten years I've known you, mate, and you never mentioned a daughter? And, I expect, a wife?"

Beryl crossed her arms. She narrowed her eyes. "If you weren't already in that bed, I'd put you there. What in the hell is wrong with you?"

Kat sat on the edge of the bed. "Tell us about her."

Andy took a deep breath and winced. "It's my business, guys. My problem and I'm not comfortable sharing."

"Hard shell, gooey centre. Tell us." Kat tapped gently on the bed. "Or your ribs are going to hurt more than they do now."

Terry nodded. "She'll do it."

Andy looked at her. He shook his head. "Nothing good ever comes of this. Personal and business shouldn't mix."

"You live in Glen Alpine. This girl is ten, right?" Beryl cocked her head. "So why were you looking for her as far south as Port Kembla and as far north as the Central Coast? She precocious enough to do that kind of travel on her own?"

"She's twelve. Almost thirteen. And that's the problem, friends. She lives in *Toul Kork*. With her mother."

Stew shook his head. "Cambodia? Jesus. You've got a secret family in Cambodia?"

"This Toul York place is in Cambodia?"

"*Toul Kork*, Terry. It's a suburb of *Phnom Penh*." Stew addressed the man in the bed. "Tell us about the secret family in Cambodia, mate. We've gotten drunk together. We've fought for each other, and *with* each other against some really bad people. I've told you things about my life and I thought you told me lots about yours, but I was clearly not worthy." He shook his head. "I trusted you."

"Mate, it's personal." He grunted as he pushed himself back up to the sitting position. "But I need your help. Obviously."

Beryl nodded. "Okay. Tell us about Kelly. And her mother."

Andy scratched at the stubble on his jaw. "Back in my SAS days. Fifteen years ago. Almost sixteen. We were doing some secret squirrel stuff in Laos. Drug interdiction for the Americans that was as black as it gets." He smiled. "Now I have to kill you all."

"Laos to Cambodia?"

"R&R. No, the mother wasn't a hooker. Half a dozen of us got into *Phnom Penh* just as some serious rain hit. There was flash flooding and we spent our R&R rescuing washed out families. Almost 24/7 for five days straight. I met Sophia, Kelly's mother, then."

"But, like, she's twelve."

"Terry, you're a genius when it comes to the guts of a computer, but you can be pretty bloody stupid." Stew hooked his thumbs in his pockets. "So you made excuses to go back there, did you? Looked her up?"

Andy smiled and fished another photo from his wallet. He handed it to Stew. "Wouldn't you?"

Stew took the small picture and held it at arm's length. "My fucking eyes. Sophia, is it?"

"Yeah."

The woman in the picture was smiling, her cheeks dimpled. Her thick chocolate brown hair was parted on the side and fell below her shoulders. The photo was from the waist up. She was wearing a loose white blouse. She looked elegant in her simplicity. Pearl drop earrings accented a gold band necklace.

"She's gorgeous. When was this taken?"

"A couple of years ago."

"She doesn't look old enough to have a twelve year old." He handed the picture back. "And why hard copies and not on your phone?"

"You fuckers get into my phone every chance you get." He

paused. "So like Stew said. For the three years I remained in the SAS I'd pop over to visit every time I had furlough. The first time it took me a while to find her, but I did.

"The first time I just checked in to make sure the family was okay. The second time I took her family out for dinner at the hotel I was staying in."

"Trying to impress the in-laws?"

"I could have saved the money. They're very well-off. Half the shirts you buy in Kmart, or Big W, or Target are made in their factory. They live very modestly."

"*Aupouk* said okay?" Stew had a schoolyard grin on his face.

"Dad was perfectly okay with the arrangement. I was going to marry her and we'd move back here."

"That didn't happen."

"You're a good detective. You should open up a place, Dan."

"So what did happen?" asked Kat.

"We compromised. In other words, she won. We got married and I bought the house in *Taul Kork*. I got out of the SAS and spent a couple of years there flogging diving trips for the tourists, back and forth to here once in a while. Mostly there, though. Almost thirteen years ago Kelly showed up. I freaked out a bit. Took off back here." He looked at Kat and Beryl's rapidly darkening faces and held up his hands. "I know. Stupid, horrible, thoughtless thing for me to do. I was an ass. I got my shit sorted when Kelly was two. Went back for a month and made up with Sophia. And her parents. Became really domesticated, but I couldn't stay there. Sophia and I came to an agreement. We love each other, and I visit as often as I can. We stay in constant communication. Kelly, Sophia and I Skype almost daily. They were planning a visit here for Christmas."

Dan cleared his throat. "The elephant in the room, Andy. Why are you looking for her here?"

Doctor Jane took this moment to break up the discussion. "Visiting hours are over. Come back tomorrow."

"No, no," said Stew. "We need fifteen more minutes."

"They stay or I check myself out, Doc. This is serious."

Jane chuckled. "You putting up with this Beryl?"

"What he said."

"Really. I could get security up here and clear all of you out in seconds." She made a decision and looked at her watch. "I'm back in fifteen with security."

Stew waited until she left. "I'm going to pay for that. So, Andy, why were you looking for her here?"

Andy rubbed his face and covered his mouth while he yawned. "Long shot. Kelly disappeared coming home from school a week ago. Sophia didn't tell me at first. Said she wasn't around when I Skyped the first couple of times, but you know me, ace detective. It took me three calls to figure out something was wrong. Man, was I pissed."

"I can imagine," said Beryl.

"I calmed down and told her I would fly there and help look. She told me that she thought Kelly was making her way here."

"She's twelve, Andy. That's nuts."

"Did you notice how much she looks like her mother?"

"Twelve. Years. Old."

"Thirteen next month, and as tall as her mother. Just as strong-willed. Sophia told me they got into a bit of a fight about the trip here. She told her mum she wanted to go now. Mum told her she had to stay until school let out for the holidays. Typical teen girl stuff. Soph couldn't find her passport and assumed she'd come here. They look a lot alike."

"You've been covering a lot of ground looking for her."

"Following the leads, as thin as they are. Sightings of ghosts of young Asian girls. And then I locked onto something else. Not sure what, but it attracted the two fucks that did this to me."

"No sign of Kelly?"

"Not a thing. But there's a smuggling operation going on. Boatloads coming in from somewhere and some kind of private auctions going on. Don't know what, but as soon as I started getting close" - he smacked the back of one hand on the other - "whack, they got me."

"Tied to Kelly, how?"

"I don't know."

Dan swore under his breath. "I don't have a good feeling about this. How did you get wind of this smuggling thing?"

"Looking for my daughter."

"And?"

Andy paled. "No."

"Human smuggling?" Kat looked at Dan, then Andy. "Are you

talking about sex-"

"NO," yelled Andy. He grabbed at the IV and tried to pull it from his arm.

Jane ran in with security. "Time to go, guys." She stuck a needle into the injection port on Andy's IV tube and depressed the plunger. "Settle down, Andy. This sedative will let you sleep. Everyone else out."

They filed into the office up the back stairs. Sat in silence for a few minutes as they gathered their respective thoughts.

"Nobody had any clue?" Beryl scanned the others' faces. "Nobody?"

Dan shook his head. "Not even a hint."

"It sure looks like his daughter has been collected by a human smuggling ring." Kat shook her head. "Completely understandable why they're fighting back as hard as they are."

Dan sat quiet, brow furrowed in thought. "This human trafficking organisation thinks we're getting close and we, honestly, have almost less than a clue. It's hard to hit back when you don't have a target. They, on the other hand, know who we are, where we are and have a very strong motivation to shut us all completely down."

"Which is why we need to get the police involved, ," said Kat. "I'm not wrong."

He shrugged. "They will be, but I'm not convinced they'll go all the way with this. We have literally no evidence other than what Andy can tell us. They'll find this Jason guy and leave it at that."

Chapter Twelve

Boots clattered up the steps. All eyes turned to the front office door. When Peters walked in, Dan said "We'll find out soon enough."

Peters stood to one side and a very pale, red-headed man in a suit and tie entered beside him. "Inspector Timothy Ryan, of the ACCCE. These are the bulk of McGinnis Investigations staff."

Dan stood and shook the men's hands. "I'm Dan McGinnis. What's that, ACCCE?"

"Australia Centre to Counter Child Exploitation." Ryan popped a stick of gum in his mouth. "Andy Smith bumped up against our investigations of a human trafficking organisation. We'd like to know what he knows."

Dan slowly moved his hand in a horizontal chopping motion for the rest of his team. "So would we. Let's move this to our conference room."

He waited until everyone was seated. "How did he 'bump up against it', if you don't mind me asking?"

"We know the two individuals who put him in the hospital. We've been keeping an eye on them."

"You saw it happen?" Kat leaned forward. "You watched them beat our friend and did nothing?"

Ryan shook his head. "We came across the two after the fact. Witnessed them loading him into the back of the ute." He held up his hand when Kat's nostrils flared and she opened her mouth. "I know what you're going to say. No, we couldn't intercede. These two are our only connection to this organisation. We're trying to find a way in, so we can take the whole operation apart."

Kat looked at Dan. *So let them know what we know?*

Dan shook his head. "How long have you been aware of this?"

"The operation itself? About a month. But human trafficking, sex trafficking has been happening for decades. Globally, about 25 million people are trapped in forced labour from this, mostly women and girls. Half are sexually exploited."

"How many in Australia?"

Ryan waggled his hand. "It's very hard to quantify. We think we get about 10% of what's going on."

"Wow," said Kat. "You are really shit at your job."

Dan stifled a smile. He leaned back and let her continue.

"I mean, if I only got 10% of my job done here, Dan would fire my sorry arse. Tax payers pay your salary, right? I wonder how many of them know how shit you are?"

Ryan's face turned red. "You clearly have no idea - "

"I mean, that ute was stolen. Didn't that twig you to something?

Ryan looked at sea. He frowned at Peters, then at Dan, and opened his mouth for a retort when Stew put his hand up.

"Don't get your panties in a bunch, Inspector. Kat likes picking fights." He narrowed his eyes. "She does make a good point though."

"Fine. We need to know what Andy has discovered to date."

"He's in the hospital right now. When we know something we'll let you know." He leaned back in his chair. "What do you have that can help us?"

Ryan shook his head and chuckled. "That's not how this works. I ask questions, you provide answers."

Dan leaned forward. "We have nothing to tell you. Maybe after Andy is able to talk. In the meantime, this is the only case we're working on." He motioned around the table. "Five of us dedicated to finding out who attacked Andy. Five of us working our way up the tree of this trafficking operation. What more can you tell us?"

The Inspector cleared his throat. "Seems fair. You just make sure to keep me in the loop, right?"

"Absolutely." Dan leaned back and crossed his arms. "What ya got?"

"This organisation seems to be active throughout the state. We think they're bringing girls in through Newcastle. Staging them at

The Entrance, or maybe Terrigal. Then they transport them to Batemans Bay, as far from the origin as possible, for the transactions."

Dan and his team looked at each other, then back at Ryan.

"Huh," said Stew. "Very interesting. The guy who beat up Andy is affiliated with this organisation?"

"Yeah. The two of them. Man and woman."

"So Newcastle, The Entrance, Terrigal and Batemans Bay?"

"Exactly."

"Okay. We'll focus our efforts there." Dan stood. "Thanks for coming by. Can you find your way out?"

"Is that it?" asked Peters.

"That's it for now."

Dan and crew waited until they heard the front door close before they spoke again.

"What's that about, boss? Why aren't we telling them what Andy told us?"

"I know you want the police to handle it, Kat, but I don't think we should be telling them everything we know."

"Why not?"

"Andy didn't ping any of those places Ryan listed. He wouldn't have been shellacked if he hadn't gone near their operations. Ryan is absolutely full of shit."

Peters stuck his head in the conference room. "Ryan's okay. A bit of a blowhard, but he seems fine."

"Wazza, you sneaky shit. What are you doing back here?"

"Your team seemed to be holding out. Look, the feds are starting to get really serious about sex trafficking. If you run into anything, let me know, okay? I can be your bridge to Ryan if you're not comfortable."

"Thanks. Now can you leave for real? We've got plans to make."

Peters smiled and held his hands up in surrender. "I'm gone. Keep me apprised, though, okay? These operations aren't run by nuns."

"Priests, maybe?"

Peters chuckled and left. Dan followed him this time to make sure he actually left.

"If we're not giving anything to the police, we should at least be getting something from them. And that was exactly nothing." Stew picked up his coffee cup and headed to the kitchen.

Beryl checked her watch. "Afternoon visiting hours have started. I'm heading back."

"We're all going. Either Andy got hit in the head harder than we think he did, or there's a real stench coming from the AFP."

.

Chapter Thirteen

Dr Jane Goulding stopped them at Andy's hospital room door. "What are you doing, Stew?"

"Let's not fight, okay? We need to confirm some information with Andy. I promise we won't wear him down."

"There's five of you. You're going to wear him down regardless how hard you try not to." She sighed. "No more than five minutes, okay? Your friend had his arse handed to him. He needs to heal."

"Five minutes. Guaranteed."

She stared at him in the eyes for a minute. "You screw him up, you get the sofa for the next week. At least."

"At least the sofa or at least a week?"

She narrowed her eyes. "Yes."

"Message received."

She stood to one side. "I'll see you tonight."

Stew pecked her on the cheek as they filed in.

"Back so soon?" Andy pushed himself up to the sitting position, with a wince and a groan. "Did I hear Jane say I had my arse handed to me?"

"Your hearing wasn't affected."

"Unkind. What's going on? Why are you back?"

"Fed visited us, with ACCCE. That's the Australia-"

"I know what it is. Cut to the chase. I'm tired."

"He told us that you've bumped into one of their operations," said Dan. "That they specifically are aware of the two individuals who, um, handed you your arse, and that they are affiliated with a human trafficking operation they are currently investigating."

"So that's great then."

"Maybe. Tell me about the places you pinged with your phone. Like Airds. Or the Hills District."

"Airds, not so sure. But there's a house in the Hills District in North West Sydney where witnesses claimed to have seen a group of under-aged girls, but only there for about a day. I also pinged Port Kembla. Whispers of a dock worker on the take, helping the smuggling operation. Why?"

"The Fed mentioned Newcastle as where they came in, and properties at The Entrance, Terrigal and Batemans Bay."

Andy frowned and shook his head. "None of those places came up on my radar."

“And you were thorough?”

He held out his arms, gesturing at the equipment he was wired up to. “What do you think?”

“So what is it?” Kat asked. “Is the Fed a moron, or is he dirty?”

Andy grunted. “Why can’t he be both?”

Chapter Fourteen

Vasily and Ilya were good at sitting. Waiting was an art, and they were artists, or so they believed.

But there were limits. They had been sitting in their beat up car, across the street from the McGinnis offices for over an hour waiting for them to leave. An hour and a half. It was getting late. The cops showing up didn't help their patience any.

Ilya looked at his watch. "We have got to go. The delivery will be coming in soon."

Vasily sighed. "I wanted to hit someone."

Ilya patted his friend on the arm and started the car. "Maybe tomorrow." He tossed his phone over. "Put the seaport address in the GPS. I always take the wrong exit." He pulled from the kerb and pointed the car toward the highway heading south.

Vasily opened an app on the phone and typed in the port. "We use Waze. For the police." He had the address half typed in when the phone rang. He looked at the caller ID. "I don't know who this is."

"Speaker phone."

Vasily pushed the button. "Da? Who is this?"

"Which one are you?" The voice was female.

Ilya leaned close to the phone. "Who. Is. This?"

"I organise logistics for the enterprise we are all part of. One of you is Ilya and the other is Vasily. You are, hopefully, at Port Kembla, preparing for cargo arrival."

"Yes," said Vasily. "We are on our way. I would tell you what time we will arrive, but we are talking on the GPS device."

"You can do both at once," said the woman.

Ilya looked at the phone, then at Vasily and shrugged.

"Less than an hour," said Vasily. "What is this? We have never had a babysitter before. We will be there."

"The cargo is two hours early. It will need to be quarantined until dark. When you say less than an hour, do you mean ten minutes or fifty-nine?"

Vasily grabbed the phone and switched apps to Waze. He pulled to the side of the road. "Hang on, logistics lady." He finished typing the address and waited for the route to calculate. "Closer to fifty-nine, I am afraid. The machine says fifty-one. If traffic goes bad, it may be longer."

The woman on the other end of the phone call swore under her breath. "I'm going to have to see if I can delay docking. Get going.

Stop for nothing. I'll let you know where the cargo is before you get there."

Jenny terminated the call. "Absolute bloody idiots." She sat in a cheaply furnished office, with Ikea furniture and thin curtains on the window. Her home office. She leaned back in her chair and covered her face. And let out a yell. Her cat jumped off the top of the file cabinet and left like its arse was dipped in kerosene then lit. She watched it go. "I feel the same way, Fritz."

She grabbed her phone and scrolled through recent calls until she found the number of the man inside at Port Kembla. A bit of cash and the occasional taste. That's all it took. It never ceased to amaze her how easy it was to corrupt a corruptible person.

Or how impossible it was to corrupt the incorruptible.

A round head, devoid of all hair except his eyebrows, and they almost compensated for the lack everywhere else, popped in the door. "What the hell was that?"

"Christophe. When did you get here?"

"A couple of minutes ago. Heard the scream from outside. The door was open. Consider it a welfare check."

"I need it. The damned Russians are still an hour out from Kembla."

Christophe looked at his watch. It was a gold Rolex almost buried in the thick hair on his arm. "No worries. Lots of time."

"Cargo is early. Two hours." She held up her phone. "I've got to try delaying it. Give me a minute."

Christophe sat in the chair across from her desk. "No problem."

She stared at him. "You need to leave the room. You can't know who I'm talking to."

"Right. Apologies. I'll be outside looking for Fritz."

"Thanks. I'll let you know when I'm finished."

She sat with her thumb hovering over the call button, waiting for him to leave and close the door behind him. It latched firmly and she tapped the screen.

"Harry here. That you, Jenny?"

"I have a problem, Harry."

"Your problem is that you won't take me up on my offer of dinner, drinking and whatever comes after that."

Jenny grimaced. "My problem is that my cargo ship is coming in early and I don't have a transfer team in place."

"The vehicle is here."

"The bus was parked there yesterday. The two morons who are supposed to facilitate the transfer and transport are almost an hour out. I need you to delay the ship's arrival."

"Hey, I'm cargo. That's harbourmaster stuff. There's nothing I can do about that."

"There's an extra couple of packets in it for you."

"No, no, no. You don't understand. If they're coming in early then they would have communicated that to the harbourmaster at least twenty-four hours ago and she would have arranged for the pilot. Those slots are like gold. You're off by more than thirty minutes it's considered cancelled and you have to provide twenty-four hours before you can come in again. So your options are two hours early or twenty-four hours late.”

Jenny clenched a fist. “Fuck. We’re already a day late.” She thought for a second. “Can you delay the cargo being offloaded?”

“Oh, hell yeah. I can slow walk it like they’re geriatric. Why?”

“My cargo can’t be offloaded until after dark. Three hours from now. That’s a lot of slow walking.”

Harry was silent. Then he cleared his throat. “It is. And it’s above and beyond. A bump would make it happen. Just a bit.”

“Cash or product?”

There was another silence. “Cash and an invitation to the auction.”

It was Jenny’s turn to be silent. She tapped a finger on her desk. “So, exactly how much cash are you expecting?”

“Triple the usual. Electronic funds transfer, same account.”

“And if I - ”

“If you don’t, the cargo gets offloaded, in broad daylight and at the *very least* you’ve lost your cargo. At the worst, it tracks back to you.”

“And you.” She clenched the phone. “I don’t like threats.”

“It would take a financial investigator years to trace money to me. I’m just doing my job. Triple in the next thirty minutes.” He hung up.

She looked out the window at the gum trees standing in her yard. It looked nice out. She needed a break. She pressed a speed dial on her phone. Samuel answered almost immediately.

"What is it?"

"I need approval for a one-time triple fee for Harry. We're in a bit of a bind. I support it, but need your sign off."

"Why the triple payment?"

"Ship is getting in two hours early. Can't delay arrival, but he can delay the cargo coming off the ship. He's got us over a barrel."

"Pay it and start grooming a replacement. Let me know as soon as you have one and I'll send Jason to Harry's house for a conversation."

Jenny shook her head. "The Russians will be down there. They like hurting people. And I've got a couple of replacements in mind."

"Did they take care of that mob sniffing around?"

"I didn't ask. It didn't seem like it."

Samuel sighed. "This is going to shit. Pay Harry and get the Russians to fix him up. Make sure they do it."

She hung up and transferred thirty thousand dollars to Harry's account. She knew that the money would stay there less than a minute before being transferred in four equal amounts to four other accounts, then repeated three more times before it ended up in his brokerage account. She had Nathan track it six months ago. It took him weeks. Harry was clever. But not smart. They'd get it back.

She sent a text to his number and called out the window. "If you've found the fucking cat, bring him in with you, Christophe."

Harry's phone vibrated on his desk, slowly shaking its way to the edge. He grabbed it and smiled. Two messages. One from his bank confirming the deposit of $30 thousand and a second from Jenny. By this time tomorrow the thirty grand would have made its way through half a dozen shell company accounts and into his brokerage account. Untraceable.

He checked the time. The ship was ten minutes from docking and clearance, which took another fifteen.

He waited, clipboard angled off his hip on one end, held in place with the crook of his wrist on the other. He waited until customs was cleared then approached the captain, a large, bearded man who looked like he was pulled from central casting. "Good voyage?"

"The usual. What do you want?" The captain looked over his head, scanning for something.

"Down here. You're looking for me." Harry tipped his head sideways and smiled. "You have a special cargo, in a special compartment in a special container. My job is to ensure that cargo gets to the right recipient at this end of the journey." He pressed open the clip on his clipboard and released an envelope. He winked and held out the clipboard like he was looking for a signature from the captain.

The captain looked at the clipboard, and the envelope, and with skills practiced over many transactions slid the envelope up his sleeve while signing a blank piece of paper.

"You'll be wanting to unload the cargo now?"

"Oh, no. Not at all. I need you to delay until dark. Can you ensure that the container in question is one of the last one off?"

The captain slid his hands in the pockets of his baggy trousers and let the envelope slide into the pocket. "They are not in a container. I have moved them to crew's quarters."

Harry sputtered. "What?" He lowered his voice and hissed. "The cargo was meant to - to be concealed. Secret." He held out his hand. "The deal is off. Give the money back or some very hard people will be visiting you."

The captain smiled. "The deal is not off. You are not getting your money back, there will be no hard people. I'm not stupid. The crew's quarters are supplemental. I never use them. On a ship such as this one we need a very small team. They each have their own quarters. The young ladies are locked in what is essentially a dormitory, sedated to the point of stupor." He wrinkled his nose. "They are beautiful, but are in need of a serious cleaning. Keep your transport team on hand until the unloading is finished for the night then move them into that bus. After that, I don't care."

Harry leaned forward. "How confident are you that the cargo wasn't discovered by your crew?"

The captain leaned just as much forward, mocking him. "One hundred percent. Now get out of my face and let me get to it."

Chapter Fifteen

Vasily slapped the steering wheel. "This is taking too long. Where are the girls?" The car was parked beside the 25 seater bus. Activity around the container ship had stopped almost an hour ago. It had been dark for thirty minutes.

"They said eight o'clock, and it's eight o'clock." Ilya shrugged. "You need to chill, mate." It sounded funny with a Russian accent, but Ilya liked it. His phone buzzed and he looked at the incoming message. An instruction from Jenny. He showed tit o Vasily and smiled. "Let me do it."

"Sure" He pointed out the windscreen. "That is Harry?"

"Da. This will be easy." Ilya pushed his large mass out of the car and leaned on the open door. "Harry, right?"

"Yeah. Let's make this fast. I'm not comfortable being in the open like this."

"Where are they?"

"On the ship. Crew's quarters. Move the bus up to the gangway and get ready."

"They are meant to be in a container, for security and secrecy. You want to walk them down a gangway, in front of everyone, with a chance that they run? Twenty-two of them? You are more stupid than you look. And you look very stupid."

Harry adjusted his shirt, pulling the front from his sweaty chest and loosening it at the shoulders. "It's not like that. They're drugged. They're barely conscious. They can walk, but they don't know where they are. And I've covered the gangway with a tent. They will be blocked from view when they come down. I'll personally escort them." He looked at his watch. "Move the bus there now." He turned and walked away, clenching and unclenching his fists.

Ilya rolled his shoulders and cracked his knuckles. "This will be really fun. You drive the bus, Vasily. I'll follow later in the car."

The girls walked down the gangway and onto the bus, escorted by Harry. Kelly was fourth down. They all had what looked like a plastic medical bracelet on their wrists, but instead of personal details, they were marked with numbers.

The bracelet on her wrist said '15'.

Harry, Ilya and Vasily made sure all of them had their seatbelts fastened. This was precious cargo. Very valuable cargo.

The last girl, a small twelve year old, was buckled into place.

Vasily checked them all one more time, then got off the bus. Harry and Ilya were standing beside the car.

Harry handed him a small notebook. "Doses and times. Very critical that the dosages - "

Vasily grabbed the book. "I know how it works. Ilya, I will meet you at the southern staging area." He looked at Harry. "Catch up when you are finished."

Ilya watched the bus pull away. The side windows were tinted. The name of a fake church community group was emblazoned on the side. He waited until it was out of sight and clapped a hand on Harry's shoulder and looked down at him. "So, Harry, you do not like the money?"

Harry shrugged the meaty hand off his shoulder. "Why-why would you say that?"

Ilya faced him and placed his hand on the back of Harry's head. He slid the hand down until his thumb and index finger was on either side of the Australian's neck. He had to push through fat before he hit resistance. "You make me nervous. I do not like that feeling."

Harry was trapped. He wanted to push away from the large Russian, but doing that forced his neck tighter in the huge hand.

Ilya squeezed harder. Harry scrambled at his hand, but the fingers were as large as sausages and the grip was steel. His eyes bulged as he scrabbled at his neck.

Ilya kept him upright with one hand while he punched him repeatedly in the body. He heard ribs snap. He pushed him up against his car and drove the heel of his work boots into each kneecap. "I cannot kill you. I am not allowed to. But that is okay to me. This is more fun."

He let go of Harry's neck and let him slump to the ground, unconscious. Technically he had met the requirements of his orders. But he was an overachiever. He stomped on both of his hands, then the forearms. Satisfying crunch noises brought a small smile to his face. He finished with similar stomps to both ankles.

He dragged Harry away from his car, dropped him on the asphalt, and drove off in pursuit of Vasily and the cargo.

The lights were off in the Airds house. Vasily pulled back the curtain on the window facing the street. He watched Ilya park the car and walk up the front steps. He opened the door for him, took a quick check of the neighbourhood, then closed and locked the door behind them. "Finished?"

"He will be out of commission for a long time. He has more broken bones than not broken bones. The girls?"

"Refreshed dosage in the food. They will be out until early morning. We will take them to the Hills then." He sniffed. "Don't want to do this by myself again. Twenty-two of them. Just me."

"You whine too much. You are confident about the dosage?"

"They are out for the night. We will have to wake them in the morning."

Ilya nodded. He yawned. "I will take the bigger sofa. See you in the morning."

Kelly was one of six in bunks, in a bedroom on the second floor. She was mostly lucid. She was exhausted, but not as drugged as the Russians thought she was.

She waited until it was quiet downstairs, then eased off the top bunk and walked to a corner as far from the others as she could. She checked the window. It was locked. Not surprisingly. Security had been good since she was grabbed on the way home from school, however many days ago that was. She bent over and stuck two of her long fingers down her throat. She retched a couple of times before her stomach spasmed and spewed the food, and drugs that were in it, onto the floor.

She checked the other girls. All of them were still out of it. She stifled a yawn and returned to the vomit. She wrinkled her nose and scooped some into the palm of her hand. She swallowed against the bile and walked into the closet. She dipped a finger in the vomit and wrote a message on the wall.

She closed the closet door, wiped her hands off on a sheet and crawled back into bed. She'd been wearing the same clothes for almost a week, as near as she could tell. She smelled like a wild ox. She fiddled with the plastic bracelet. The number was starting to fade. She'd ripped it off when she was on the ship and was told if she did it again she'd have to swim the rest of the way.

All of the drug didn't come up with the vomit. She was tired. She closed her eyes, knowing that she wouldn't be in this situation for long.

Chapter Sixteen

Terry was talking to Kat and Beryl was talking to Stew, then Stew would bark something at Terry and the cacophony was giving Dan a headache. They were at the office, in the conference room.

Dan held up his hands. "Enough, for fuck's sake. One at a time." He pointed. "Beryl."

"We absolutely have to do this."

"I don't think you'll find anyone here disagrees. But we can't follow Terry's plan and — what was it you said? Bust some fucking heads? We need a better plan that that. They put Andy in a bed, we have to be smarter than them."

Kat shrugged. "At least smarter than Andy."

Dan nodded. "Common sense says we hit the port first thing in the morning."

"Why not now?"

"Because it's fucking dark out, I'm buggered," said Stew. "We all need rest or we'll make stupid mistakes."

Dan pointed. "What he said. Stew and I will head to Port Kembla in the morning. Terry, you and Kat check out the Airds location. See what you can see. Be careful. It didn't look occupied when we were there earlier. That doesn't mean it still isn't."

Beryl knocked on the table. She looked tired, her hair out of place and bags under her eyes. "What am I doing?"

"You're staying with Andy. Let him know we're doing everything we can. And you need to get some rest tonight. You look terrible."

"I will cut you."

Dan laughed. "You're tougher than all of us, but these guys are mean. I don't want you hurt. You're better with Andy. He needs to stay in the hospital until Dr Jane says he can leave, or he'll be no good to any of us." He sighed. "I know you've got an itch to be in the middle of things, but it's not safe for you. And my team's safety is my absolute, number one concern."

"So, um, what are Kat and I doing in Airds? I'm no Andy. And Kat, I know she fights dirty, but still." He smiled at Kat, but looked nervous.

Kat pushed away from the table. "All this talk is bullshit. Beryl, can you put a site together for a solar panel company? I'll make up some brochures. We'll go door to door, starting a couple of houses away. If there's someone in the house, we do our pitch. If there's nobody there, we break in and take a look."

Dan smiled. "Best hire I've made yet. Beryl, this is an easy website, right?"

"Fifteen minutes."

"Stew and I are going to need IDs to get on the port grounds without a hassle."

Kat interjected. "I'll make them. Then I'll put the brochures together and email you a copy. Do the site tomorrow, Beryl. Terry and I will start door knocking at 10. I'm beat."

Dawn comes early in Australia's November. The room started getting light around 5:30 and by 5:45 Kelly could see the other girls, all nearly comatose. She heard footsteps in the hallway and closed her eyes. She'd figured out how to avoid most of the drugs two days ago. She was in Australia. She knew that. Where, she wasn't so sure. But she knew Andy was in Australia and it didn't matter how big the country was, he'd find her or she'd find him.

The door opened. She cracked an eyelid and watched the skinny one come in and slap the bottom of the other girls' feet. She thought his accent was Russian. It sounded Russian. She groaned as he approached her bed and pretended to wake up. "Where are we?"

He ignored her and smacked the girl on the bottom bunk on the soles of her feet with a riding crop. "Everybody get out of bed and stand. Do you understand? If you understand what I am saying, tell the others who maybe do not."

She stood beside the other girls. When he grabbed her wrist to read the number she asked, "Do you know where we are?"

He slapped her. "You shut mouth."

She rubbed the side of her face. It wasn't a hard slap. She'd been hit harder, before, by others. She took a breath, contemplating an attack, when the big one walked in. She let out her breath and relaxed back in line.

The big one had bag of water bottles with numbers written on them. He grabbed her wrist, read the number and handed her a bottle. "Drink all of it. Now. No stopping."

She twisted off the cap, threw it across the room and drank the water, letting some of it spill over her chin and onto her blouse. But she knew she wouldn't be able to divert enough. She'd be out this time.

She threw the bottle at the big one. She had a pretty good idea they couldn't, or wouldn't, hurt her. She was wanted for something else. She didn't want to think too much about it.

The heaviness hit almost immediately. Her thoughts slowed. Her tongue was thick and she watched her hands like they were someone else's.

She hated this part.

Vasily escorted the six from Kelly's room down to the side door of the house. The others were already there, sixteen drugged and compliant girls. Six more made twenty-two. Ilya backed the bus up the drive until the door was beside the stairs to the house. He waited until Vasily opened the side door and pulled on the handle to open the bus door.

Vasily marched them into the bus, moving them to the back and filling it to the front. He made sure they were all buckled in. Precious cargo. He walked to the back and checked each of them again. There would be a nice bonus in this.

He leaned on the railing by the front door. "We are ready to go. You have the address?"

"Da. I am not a child."

"Remember, do not speed, do not go too slow. I will drive ahead. If there is a roadside stop with police I will let you know. Pull over immediately on a side street and wait thirty minutes. They never last longer than that."

"Yes, yes, shut up and go."

Kat parked her car a block from the house in question. It was a clear day, warm already at 9:30 in the morning. An overnight rain had scrubbed the place clean and left the plant life green, but Kat still wrinkled her nose at the surroundings. "I've got a rule about where I live."

"Yeah? What rule is that?" Terry riffled a stack of glossy three-fold brochures extolling the virtues of roof mounted solar panels.

"When the yards are fenced, like they are around here, fences and gates and a general unwelcoming vibe, I stay away. Especially these ugly chain link fences."

"Well, it's not the greatest of neighbourhoods." He handed her the brochures. "I grew up about a block from here. Shit neighbourhoods don't guarantee shit people."

"Jury's still out."

"Oh, fuck you very much," he smiled. He opened the car door. "Let's do this."

Stew looked up from the map on his phone. "You know where we're going?"

Dan pointed to a sign ahead of them. "Left at the lights. Inner harbour." He waited for a break in traffic and pulled through. "Get out your ID." He grabbed his from behind the visor. "Gate ahead."

Stew flicked at the edge of his laminated card, identifying him as an employee of the Australian Maritime Safety Association. "Hate this picture."

"A good picture on an ID is a sure sign of it being a fake." Dan rolled up to the gate and held his card out the window. He barely stopped as the guard glanced at the familiar colours and patterns on the card and raised the boom gate.

Stew looked over his shoulder as the guard hut disappeared behind them. "Don't tell Kat they didn't even look at them, okay? Might not go over well."

"I won't if you won't. Where from here?"

Stew looked out the window, orienting the map on his phone with the surroundings. "Stay straight past all these cars."

Hundreds of brand new Toyotas, waiting for a new home, stretched out from the road a dozen deep. A car-carrier truck pulled out of the lot in front of them and hit the round-about, turning back the way Dan and Stew had come.

"Go straight through and continue on a bit."

More cars lined the left of the road. New, wax on the windscreens and plastic cling on the door handles. Stew pointed at a small parking lot beside a huge metal roofed warehouse. "Turn right, there." A container ship was berthed and big men in work clothes were milling around it.

Dan parked and exhaled. He reached into the backseat and retrieved a fluoro-yellow vest and a hard hat. "Look professional."

Stew exited with the same outfit and a clipboard. "Right behind you."

Dan pulled open the door into the container offices harder than necessary. Stew grabbed it before it hit the wall.

"Who's in charge?" Dan looked around. It wasn't a large office, maybe twelve desks. Bodies at eight of them. Five women and three men. One of the older women stood with a frown and beckoned them over.

'I'm Pearl. What's the fuss, barging like this?"

They sat across from her and placed their hardhats on her desk.

Dan held out his identification. "Dan Fielding. AMSA. Safety division. We received a tip that there was a stowaway, maybe more than one, on a container ship that docked recently."

"That's a job for immigration, isn't it?"

Stew leaned forward. "They're doing their part. We're more concerned about the safety side of the equation. A stowaway contemplates a civilian, with no personal protection equipment, wandering through the docks. Most likely at night. The safety hazards, well…" Stew threw up his hands. "I can't even think about how many forms I'd have to fill out."

Dan bit the inside of his cheek trying not to smile.

"You're kidding, right?" Pearl looked confused. "What do you expect us to do? Have an easy access closet with PPE sitting out on the docks just in case there are stowaways?"

Stew nodded. "That's the kind of thinking I like. We have to think outside the box when it comes to safety."

Dan, sitting slightly behind Stew caught Pearl's eyes, raised his eyebrows and shrugged. He rested his hand on Stew's shoulder. "Look, I realise you probably have no idea about this stowaway. Who is best to talk to about incoming container ships?"

"Containers are a small part of our business. Lots of RoRo car ships, coal exports, bulk liquid. Containers are like less than 10 percent."

"Containers are the most likely, though. Not likely to have a stowaway on a coal shipment, are we?" Dan smiled. "Who's the best contact? Don't need to take up any more of your valuable time."

"Last night was it?"

"That's our most reliable information."

Pearl grunted and wrote in block letters on a Post-It note. "Harry Ford. Except he's in the hospital. Good luck talking to him. He was beat up last night sometime. In a right shit shape."

Dan and Stew looked at each other. "Who did it?" asked Dan.

Pearl shook her head. "No clue. He was found unconscious this morning in the middle of the parking lot. Looked real bad." She frowned. "You think your stowaway did this?"

"Possible. What hospital?"

She looked at him like he was the slow child. "Wollongong Hospital. Loftus Street. Where else?"

Dan nodded. "Thanks for your assistance, Pearl."

Stew grabbed the hardhats off her desk and handed one to Dan. "Thanks for your cooperation in this important matter."

Dan held the door for him, nodded at Pearl and left. "Forms?" he asked when they got outside.

"Typical officious, illogical bureaucrat, boss."

They trotted to the car. "Who do you think did Harry?"

Dan shook his head, getting the hospital address set up in the mapping app on his phone. "The usual suspects, I guess. Let's go see if he can talk."

Terry and Kat walked side-by-side down the path from the front door to the gate of the house beside their target house, another lead gathered for a potential solar customer. Terry stood to one side and held the gate open. "We should change careers. We could make a killing with solar panels."

"It's the quality of the brochures, hey?" She nodded at the next house. "This is it. Looks empty."

"With any luck."

"You're a bit of a wuss, aren't you?"

Terry raised his eyebrows and cocked his head. "Look at me? Not

Andy. Definitely not Stew. I'm the guy with the electronics who sorts stuff out in the back room. I'm barracking for an empty house."

"I think you've lucked out, then." Kat knocked on the door while Terry peered through the front window.

Up close the paint was fading and peeling, the windows were filthy and spiderwebs filled the corners.

"This place is a shit hole," said Kat. "Nobody's home."

Terry looked around. "Check the back."

They walked around the side of the house and up the drive. Terry tapped her on the arm and pointed. "Check it out."

"What?"

"Oil drops. On the driveway. Still wet. They soak in pretty quick. Someone was here this morning."

"You going to tell me the make and model from the oil, slick?"

Terry chuckled. "Not quite." He handed her a pair of latex gloves. "Put these on." He snapped on a pair himself and tried the doorknob on the side of the house. It turned and he slowly pushed the door open. "Shit."

"We go in?"

Terry shrugged. "We're here. Why not?"

She leaned her head in, craning her neck to look on the walls beside the door. "No alarm, thank God."

"Let's go then. In quick and close the door before anyone notices." Terry followed Kat in, closed the door behind him and threw the deadbolt.

They stood still and surveyed the layout. They were standing in the kitchen. A laundry room was to the immediate right. There were no appliances in the laundry room, just a large, deep sink and a hot water tank.

There was a fridge in the kitchen. Terry pulled open the door. There were a couple of bottles of water and a beer in the door. Nothing else. "Nobody lives here. It's a way station."

Kat nodded and pointed to plastic wraps on the floor beside an unopened flat of 500ml bottles of water. "Three flats of water. Not refrigerated. Two used. That's a lot, considering there's no food."

They walked carefully into the living area. "No television. What kind of place is this?"

"An overnight stop," said Kat. "And they slept on the sofa?"

Two sofas on either side of the living area had blankets thrown across them in a mess. Pillows were at one end of each of them.

"I'm checking upstairs," said Terry.

"Right behind you."

A hall extended from the top of the stairs. There were three doors on each side of the hallway. Terry pushed one of them opened. "Loo."

Kat opened door on the opposite side. "Check this out." She wrinkled her nose. "Stinks of sick in here."

Three sets of bunkbeds were crammed into the small room. All six beds looked slept in. "Guards slept downstairs. Captives up here."

Terry ran across the hall and opened the other two doors. "Two sets of bunks in these."

Kat checked the other two. "Two each in these ones, too." She thought a second. "Beds for twenty two. And two guards."

"They would have drugged whoever was in these beds. Twenty-two against two is an easy fight, otherwise."

Kat nodded. "That's what the water was for. Made them drink something before they left. They're in a bus of some sort."

"Heading farther north."

"How do you figure?"

Terry smiled. "They came in at Port Kembla. Stopped here overnight because they didn't want to go the full run. It's only an hour from the port. They're probably heading to somewhere north of the city."

"Not bad, detective boy."

"Let's look around and see if we can find something."

Kat snorted. "There's beds and sheets. No food. They came in last night and left in the morning. We're not going to find anything."

"We're going to look. Someone could have dropped something. I'll start here." He walked into the room with three sets of bunks. "Call out if you see something."

"Hey, what happens if someone comes back? We're trapped upstairs."

"Be fast, then. I doubt they will."

He pulled sheets back off the thin mattresses, checked under the beds. He was by the window and caught himself just about to step in a pool of drying vomit. "Found it."

Kat called from across the hall. "Found what?"

"The smell. Someone puked."

"Lucky you." Her voice faded as she made her way down the hall.

Terry grunted and squatted by the drying vomit. It looked like someone had made a half-hearted attempt at cleaning it up. He stood and took a closer look at the sheets. Brownish streaks on one of the upper bunk looked a little like the sick. But there wasn't enough to make up for what looked like was missing from the floor.

He pulled back the thin curtains to expose the windows and window frames. Dirty, with cobwebs. He continued, checking the walls, the bed frames. He didn't find what he was looking for.

He turned on the torch on his mobile phone and stepped into the closet. On the inside wall, close to the doorframe, someone had used the vomit to write some words with their finger. The edges of the letters weren't clear, and faded where the finger ran out of 'ink'.

"Kat, get in here." He took a couple of pictures and stepped out of the closet. He edited the photos to contrast the letters against the wall as much as possible.

Kat looked over his shoulder while he worked. "Where was that?"

Terry pointed at the closet and finished editing. He sent the photo to Stew, Dan, Beryl and Kat then followed her into the closet. She was playing her phone light over the writing on the wall. "That says what I think it does, right?"

Kat nodded. "*Andy Smith McGinnis*. Damn."

Terry sent a copy of the picture to the group text chain. "We've got to get back to the office. Now."

Chapter Seventeen

Dan and Stew left the fluoro vests and hardhats in the car before they entered the A&E department. Stopped at the admissions counter. "Looking for a Harry Ford. Patient came in on a stretcher very early this morning, beaten to a pulp."

The nurse typed some commands on her terminal "Yeah, he came in in bad shape. Got out of surgery a couple of hours ago. What's this about?"

They held out their fake identification cards. "AMSA. Got some questions for him related to an incident on an arriving cargo ship. His beating may have been part of what happened. Is he able to be visited?"

"That's awkward phrasing. Yes, visiting hours are now and you can try." She scribbled a room number on a piece of paper. "Visiting hours are, however, over in about twenty minutes, so you don't have much time."

Harry was conscious, but in a number of casts. Stew and Dan pulled up chairs beside his bed.

"Looks bad, Dan."

Dan shrugged. "No concussion. He'll talk."

Harry looked at them. "Who the hell are you guys?"

"It's about stowaways on cargo ships. We've been led to believe you're the man to talk to about that."

He paled. Swallowed, and looked nervously at the door.

Stew got up and closed the door and returned to his chair. "You seem nervous."

He glanced back at the door and cleared his throat. "Jesus Christ. How did you guys find out about it?" He stopped. "Those fucking Russians. Did they send you?"

"What can you tell us?"

"Am I under arrest? No, you're not cops. What the fuck are AMSA looking at Russians for?"

"We need to know about the stowaways. If there is going to be any police action it will be independent of us." Stew looked at his clipboard, made a meaningless scribbling motion.. "When did they come in?"

"Last night. You don't know?"

"Working on a tip. All details need to be confirmed. On a container ship, right?"

"It's been loaded and gone by now."

"We're not looking for it. We're looking for the stowaways."

"The fucking Russians. I already told you. Last night."

"Listen," said Dan. "This is very important. Where did they go?"

"I don't fucking know. That's not my piece of the puzzle. I get a call that there's a bunch coming in and I facilitate the transfer." Sweat pooled in the hollow of his throat. His hair was plastered to his head. "They said I'd never get into trouble. Jesus. It was just for the money."

Stew grabbed Harry's arm just above the cast and squeezed. Hard. "Just the money, hey?" He applied more pressure until Harry started whimpering.

"Jesus, Jesus let go fuck that hurts oh fuck oh fuck."

"Where did they go?"

'North. I don't know anything more than that."

"The Russian's names?"

"Vasily, the small one and the big guy, Ilya. They drove an old Corolla. Someone had left a 25 seater bus in the parking lot the day before. They loaded the girls on the bus and left around ten last night."

"A bus? How many girls were there?"

"Eighteen, twenty, Jesus let go of my arm."

Stew and Dan's phone pinged in unison. They both checked the message and looked at each other.

Stew nodded and stood. "Talk to anyone about our conversations and I'll be back and you'll wish you'd never met me."

They left the hospital at a trot.

Stew got behind the wheel. "You see the picture just Terry sent?"

Dan nodded. "How fast can we get back?"

"So the question we need to address right now is how much do we tell the police," said Beryl. Prints of the photo were spread across the conference room table. "Was there anything else in the Airds house?"

Kat shook her head. "Almost nothing in that place. It was a stopping place. No long term stay. No food. No amenities. Not even a television."

"Forget the police. Do we tell Andy?" asked Terry.

"We can't 'forget the police'. This is a federal crime. Human trafficking. Jesus." Dan scrubbed his face. "How many beds?"

"Twenty-two. Most of them looked like they were used. A couple dozen bottles of water gone."

"Fuck." He sighed and looked at Kat and Terry. "Your prints are all over the place, aren't they?"

Kat smiled. "No, Terry made us wear protection."

"He's learning." Dan held up the photo. Andy's name, and his. "This writing was in an out of the way place?"

"In the closet, on the side wall close to the closet door hinges. No way you'd find it if you weren't looking for it."

"This is clear, right? His daughter is in that group," said Dan. "Nobody else in the world would be in that house with the knowledge of Andy's name and my name, and would write it in puke in an out of the way place in a closet. Right?"

"Quit beating the horse. It's dead. You're right. And yes, we need to tell Andy."

"You sure, Beryl? He'll check himself out early and want to be in the thick of it. I don't think he's ready."

She looked at the picture again. "No, you're probably right."

"I'll give Peters a call. Tomorrow. I want us to check a couple of things first."

"Central Coast," said Stew.

Dan nodded. "You and I. Call Mac and let him know you're on your way back." He pointed at Terry. "You and Kat are on a roll. Head to the Hills district, that other place that Andy pinged. The farm. See what you can see. Beryl, hold the fort."

She waved her hand. "Just an old lady sitting in the office, nothing to do."

Dan raised his eyebrows. "None of that." He checked the time. "We need to leave now. You two," he looked specifically at Terry, "be careful. These people aren't nice and have a lot to lose."

"All four of you check in regularly," insisted Beryl.

"And put some serious hurt on whoever is running this shit show."

"Easy, Terry. That's after. And we will. Be ready." He clapped his hands together. "Let's go."

Beryl watched them leave, a sinking feeling in her chest. She checked the list of numbers on her desk and dialled.

"Peters."

"Hey, Wazza. Beryl here. You got a minute?"

"For you, always. What kind of trouble has Dan got himself into now?"

"That's the thing. Andy's assault has taken a very dark turn. I think we may need to talk to Ryan again. It'll have to be tomorrow. Dan and Stew are up on the Central Coast and Terry and Kat are in the Hills District. All of them doing some surveillance. They all should be here for this."

"Surveillance. Why am I having a tough time believing that?"

Beryl shrugged. "I don't control your thoughts."

Peters laughed. "How's Andy doing?"

"He's recovering quickly. He's got a hard head."

"I heard Stew got a lick in with two of them, too."

"How'd you hear that?"

"The servo owners in Airds saw a bit of it. Your boy Stew is no slouch. It was all self-defence, so we're not pursuing him for anything."

Beryl sat forward. "Did you pick up the two he fought?"

"They were gone by the time the local cops showed up."

"Well they're the foot soldiers. Hate to think how bad they get farther up the tree." Beryl checked the time. "I'll let you know when the crew is back in town. We can come to you, or you and your federal friends can come here. I make good coffee."

"Waiting for your call, Beryl."

Chapter Eighteen

Beryl drummed her fingers on her desk. A couple of months prior she was neck deep in one of the most dangerous cases she'd ever been involved in, and the adrenaline rush proved to be addictive.

Sitting in the office didn't quite cut it anymore.

She heard the door at the bottom of the stairs open and light footsteps climb the stairs. Her desk faced the office door. Most times the steps walked past to the neighbouring accountants office, but this time they stopped. A brief hesitation and the door pushed open. A slight woman, Asian, with long, thick, dark brown hair slowly stepped in.

"Mr McGinnis is here?"

"Mr McGinnis isn't. My name is Beryl. What can I do for you?"

"I am looking for Andy Smith. He said he works at McGinnis Investigations. Is Andy here?"

Beryl put the pieces together in about half a second. She stood and reached out her hand. "You must be Sophia. My goodness, come here. Your picture doesn't do you justice. When did you get here?"

"Andy is here?"

"You better sit down. Let me get you some water." Beryl showed her to a sofa in the waiting area, disappeared and returned seconds later with a bottle of cold water.

"People tell me to sit down when there is a problem. Is Andy okay?"

"He'll be fine. He's a strong boy. He's the hospital right now - " she rested her hand on Sophia's arm, stopping her from standing. "It's okay. I think he'll be out tomorrow. He was looking for your daughter and got himself in a bit of trouble."

Sophia grabbed Beryl's hand with both of hers. "He found Kelly?"

"He hasn't. But we're all working on it. All of us. The entire office. Dan - Mr McGinnis - and all of the rest of us."

Sophia sagged. "It's been too long. Kelly is strong, but it has been too long. I need to see Andy."

"Let me call Dan. He needs to get back here. We'll go together." She sent a text message and received an almost immediate response. "He'll be back in thirty minutes. Do you need food? You have to tell me what happened with Kelly."

"I can't eat. We need to find my daughter."

Beryl took her hands and held them firmly. "We are. Full court press. Anything you can tell me about how Kelly was taken may help." She let go of Sophia's hands and turned the voice memo recorder on. "So you don't have to say it twice."

Sophia took a deep breath. "How much do you know?"

"Nothing, really. I didn't know you and Kelly existed until yesterday. None of us did. And we only discovered that when Andy surfaced after a week away, severely beaten up."

"Andy was beaten up? No. That's not right."

"I know. Surprised us, too. We're up against a really serious crowd."

Sophia looked hard in Beryl's eyes. "How serious is *your* crowd? I'll do this myself if I have to, but I don't know the country, and I'm just one."

"Andy is family. That makes you and Kelly family. And we will do anything for family. When did Kelly disappear and why did you think she came here?"

"A little over a week ago she didn't come home from school. I don't know if she disappeared on the way there, during the day, or on the way home." She held her face in her hands. "I'm really upset that I don't even know that. I called the local police, but they just assumed she was a runaway and didn't do anything."

Beryl nodded sympathetically. "In my experience, police aren't much help in matters like these."

"Yes. I wasted two days checking with her friends and trying to convince the police to look for her. And then I noticed that my passport was missing, and Kelly had been pestering me to come here to visit her father. I assumed she went here."

"She was - is - only twelve."

"She *is* a tall, stubborn, smart girl. Thirteen. Not twelve." She laced her fingers together, twisting them, displaying her nerves. "Then, two days after I told Andy the story I found my passport. The police found her schoolbag in a garbage bin on the route from school to home. I - I don't understand why Andy was beaten up, or why it's taking so long finding Kelly. What aren't you telling me?"

"Do you drink? Alcohol?" Beryl stood.

"It's not even noon."

Beryl nodded and poured two cups of coffee. Added a splash of whiskey to both and handed Sophia one of them. "There are legitimate exceptions to every rule. Drink."

Sophia took the cup and placed it to one side. "Talk to me, Beryl."

"If you won't, I will." Beryl took a mouthful of the spiked coffee and sighed. "Andy believes he's run into a human trafficking ring while searching for your daughter. It seems like she didn't run away. It seems like she was grabbed by a trafficking ring and brought here."

Sophia looked at her for a minute, then took the cup of coffee and drank. "I knew it." She shook her head. "No, I didn't know it, but I worried about it. It happens in Cambodia a lot, but usually it's poorer girls, sent here to find a better life, then held in virtual slavery." She took another drink. "This sounds worse than that."

"It may be. But trust me when I say we have dropped every other case we're working on and we're devoting the entire team to this, and only this."

Sophia looked around the office. "I want to see Andy. Can you take me there?"

Andy hovered between sleep and consciousness. He had dialled back the pain meds as much as he could bear. Opiates dulled him. He shifted in the bed and the sharp pain of a cracked rib brought him fully awake.

Standing in front of him was a vision of his wife. "I'm dreaming." He thumbed the control on the morphine drip to reduce the flow even more. "Hallucinating."

"No, hun, that's Sophia. She's come looking for you. Wondering why you're just lying around."

"When your daughter is still missing," said Sophia. She crossed her arms. "You rested enough?"

"You're really here?" He reached out, wincing.

Sophia stepped closer, smiling. She took his hand and squeezed. "Are you okay?"

"I'll be fine. Why did you come?"

"Don't be stupid. And stubborn. Like you always are. This is our daughter. I have just as much right to look for her as you do."

"Of course you do. Of course." Andy adjusted himself and winced. "I'm not ready to leave here yet. I want to, that's for damned sure. But I'm not as stupid as I look. I don't want you going off on your own. Stick with Beryl and the team and don't go feral on me, okay?"

"I'm not stupid either, stupid man." She frowned. "Is Kelly okay?"

"How much do you know?"

Sophia looked at Beryl who nodded. "It's most likely that our daughter has been caught up in a sex trafficking ring. She's going to be sold to some pervert. We're not too late, are we?"

Andy waved his hands over his body. "They wouldn't beat the shit out of me if the sale had already been completed. We still have a little time, I think."

"The girls arrived this morning," said Beryl. "Very early morning. We found a message in a house not far from here that your daughter left inside of a closet. She wrote with her vomit. She's a very resourceful young lady."

"She gets that from me," Sophia and Andy replied in unison.

Andy chuckled and groaned. "We still have a couple of days. Beryl, where is everybody?"

"They were heading in pairs to the Hills District and the Central Coast. I've called them back to meet and talk to Sophia."

Andy grunted. "Thanks." He winced. "Jane is going to be here in a minute to chase you all out."

Sophia leaned in and kissed Andy. "I missed you."

Andy smiled. "Not as much as I missed you. We need to discuss how we go forward once we get our daughter back."

"Yes."

Dr Jane leaned in the room. "Do I need muscle?"

Beryl held up her hands. "We're going. Thanks for allowing us to in." She plucked at Sophia's arm. "Let's go, hun."

Sophia smiled at Andy. "Do what the good doctor tells you or she has my permission to slap you around."

Terry and Kat were already at the office when Beryl returned with Sophia.

Kat hugged Sophia, then held her out at arm's length. "Your arsehole husband never mentioned a word about you. Do I have permission to hit him once he's out of the hospital?" She pulled her in for another hug.

"For god's sake, Kat. Let the poor woman breathe."

"Andy talked about you, Kat." She looked at Terry, who was standing back. "You too, Terry. It's very nice to meet you."

Terry nodded and smiled. "You too. He said absolutely nothing about you. Frankly, it's both a huge shock, and not really a surprise. Andy's a very private man."

Dan leaned on the kitchen door and chuckled. "That's an understatement. How are you, Sophia? Your picture doesn't do you justice."

"You are Dan." Sophia looked up at him earnestly. "Have you found Kelly yet?"

"Considering we had no idea she, or you, existed prior to yesterday, no. We're doing the best we can. We were heading north to check some places Andy had pinged while he was searching."

"So you're back at ground zero? Why don't you talk to Andy and find out what he's done already?"

"We did. He's nowhere. The only clue we had that he was getting close was the enormous beating he took. We know he was getting close, but not what he was getting close to. So we retrace his steps."

Stew pushed in. "Great to meet you, Sophia. We'll share stories later, okay? Like the boss said, we have steps to retrace. We're almost an hour behind schedule and a long way to travel."

"Of course. I'll start here and pick Beryl's brains while you find my daughter." She shook her head. "Are you kidding me? I'm going with you."

Beryl put her arm around her shoulders. "I know you think you need to, but you saw what these people did to your husband. We'll stay here. You give me as much information as you can think of and I'll relay it to the team. And you must be exhausted."

Dan checked the time. "You know what? I think our time would be better served if we stayed here and talked to Sophia, share with her where we are and get as much information about her daughter as possible. By the time we get up to the Central Coast it'll be near dark. Not a good use of our time."

Chapter Nineteen

Kat double checked that the apartment door was locked. "Incipient OCD, I think." She pushed open the front door and smiled. It was another beautiful day. Talking with Sophia the night before had made things seem more possible. The walk to the office was less than a kilometre, just enough to wake her up. She walked through Mawson Park and cut through the parking lot behind the chicken place. It reminded her of the young girl. She briefly wondered how she was doing and if, maybe, she should talk to Dan about using the girl's case as the one she could lead. Her first solo case.

She was walking past a pile of refuse made up mostly of cardboard boxes when a rustling noise from underneath made her jump sideways.

"Fucking snakes." She peered warily at the pile, like cardboard shale. She held her phone close to her mouth. "Hey, Siri, find a snake wrangler near me."

"Just a tick." Siri paused. "I found these on the internet."

She glanced at her phone, then jumped again when a muffled whimper emanated from the pile.

She dropped her phone in her bag, and her bag on the ground and started pulling pieces of cardboard out of the way, a snake wrangler the furthest thing from her mind. A hand was exposed when she lifted the third piece, then the rest of the young girl from the restaurant. She was in bad shape. Her face was bloody and bruised. Her arm was bent in an unnatural direction and one of her legs was clearly broken.

Kat suppressed the urge to vomit and scrambled through her bag for her phone. "Hi, I need an ambulance and probably police. I've just found a badly beaten girl." She provided the address. "In the large parking lot in behind." She looked around to get her bearings. The back entrance to the restaurant was about thirty metres west. "The fuckers."

"Excuse me?"

"Never mind. Send someone fast."

"Stay on the phone. Is she breathing?"

"Yes." Kat leaned close. "It's shallow, but she's breathing. She isn't conscious, I don't think."

"Does her breathing sound wet?"

"Can you just for fuck's sake send somebody?"

"I've already dispatched, dear. Stay on the line. Everything you're telling me I'm relaying to the ambo so they're ready when they get there. Is her breathing wet?"

Kat pulled the phone from her head. She could hear sirens. "Sorry. She just looks really bad. Yes, it kind of gurgles. I shouldn't move her, should I?"

"Correct. Do you know who did this? Are you safe right now?"

Kat looked at the restaurant. "No I don't know, and yes I am."

"What injuries can you see?"

"Her face is really beaten up. A lot of blood. Her arm looks like either her shoulder is dislocated or something is broken and she has a compound fracture on her lower leg. Tibia or fibula. I can never remember which one."

"That's great. You're doing great. The ambulance should be almost there."

On cue, the van pulled into the parking lot, cut the siren and rolled to a stop beside her. The two paramedics jumped out.

"You called this in?"

Kat stood and got out of the way and pointed. "They just got here," she said into the phone.

"You were great. I'll leave you with them."

She pocketed her phone and stood behind the ambulance attendants as they placed a backboard beside the girl.

"Do you know her name? We couldn't find any identification on her."

She shook her head. "I was walking to work when I heard a

whimpering noise. I found her about five minutes ago."

The other attendant was relaying information to the hospital through her radio. She waved her partner over. "Doesn't look like there's a back problem. Got reflexive action. Let's get her moved. I think there's internal bleeding."

"I'm coming with her."

"Weren't you on the way to work?"

"My boss will understand." Kat typed a quick message to Dan. "I don't want her waking up alone."

"Fine with me. Just stay out of my way." He looked over her shoulder, past her. "Those guys are going to want to talk to you, too."

She turned and watched a police car pull into the lot and stop beside the ambulance. "Not much I can tell them."

"They'll still want to know what you know." He glanced at his partner who was waiting for him. "We're going to be about another ten minutes. If you're finished with them before we leave, travel with us. If not, we're going to the Campbelltown hospital. She'll be checked in under Jane Doe."

Sr Constable Warren stepped out of the car and pulled a notepad from somewhere inside his utility vest. "I'm Sr Constable Paul War
_ "

"I know. We've met. Make sure your body cam is on."

He poised his pencil poised over the pad. "Your name?"

"Kat. Katherine Brady. I work for Dan McGinnis."

He smiled and nodded. "Right. At the Andy thing. What happened here?"

"Don't know. I was walking to the office and heard her whimper under the cardboard."

"Any idea what her name is?"

Kat glanced at the restaurant. "She had no i.d. on her. I don't know what her name is." She looked at the pair working to get her on the backboard and stabilised. "Hey, I want to travel with her in the ambulance, okay? I don't want her to wake up and be alone."

He stuffed the notepad back from whence it came. "No problem. I know where to find you if I need to." He adjusted his vest. "The homeless problem is getting bad."

"No, she wasn't homeless."

"Well, we'll determine that."

"She was too well dressed. And too young. She isn't more than fifteen."

"Hard times hit all of us once in a while. They key is to have a good support structure around you." He patted her on the head. "You ride with her. I'll catch up with you later."

He slid back into his car and flipped off the lights. He rolled out, speaking something on the mic. He nodded at Kat as he drove past her.

She rubbed the top of her head. "I'm really starting to hate that guy."

The paramedics carefully lifted the girl onto the backboard, strapped her down and placed her, and the board, on the gurney. They slid her into the back of the ambulance and locked her down.

"Susie, watch the bumps. I'm going to be doing what I can back here."

The guy stayed in the back and Susie got out and held the door. Kat pulled herself into the back and sat opposite the guy. "I'm Kat. She's Susie. What's your name?"

"Keith. Remember your promise."

Kat sat back and held her hands up. "Right. I stay out of your way."

Susie closed the back doors and Kat felt the ambulance shift as she got behind the wheel. Kat adjusted herself as they started moving. The siren started just as Kat's mobile rang.

She pressed the phone against her head and jammed a finger on the opposite ear. "Kat speaking."

"Just got your message. Sounds like you're in an ambulance. Is it the same girl?"

"Yeah. It's pretty bad."

"You're going with her to the hospital?"

"I have to."

"Wouldn't expect anything different. I'm going to go by and have a chat with the guy at the restaurant."

"Maybe don't." She glanced at Keith. "Let me look into it."

Dan was quiet for a minute. "Look, I don't want you to get hurt like she did. You should start off with something lighter."

"You didn't see her."

"I know. I'll stay away from the guy. Today. But you stay away from him, too. We're going to talk later and figure out what to do."

"Thanks, boss."

The siren stopped and a flurry of activity at the back door of the ambulance pulled the girl on the gurney and moved her rapidly into the A&E. Keith placed a hand on her arm. "Wait here. You can't go in. I'll let them know you're an interested party and waiting for her condition."

"Thanks. You think she'll be okay?"

"She's going to need surgery. There's some internal bleeding. I don't know how bad, but it could be serious."

Kat chewed the inside of her cheek and gave him a weak smile. "Thanks. Let me give you my mobile number."

"Don't blame you for not wanting to hang around." He handed her a pad and pen.

"I've got a friend in here." She wrote her number and name. "I'll stop by and kill some time with him."

"You live a fun life."

"Don't I, though. Thanks again."

Kat poked her head in Andy's hospital room. "Safe to come in?"

Sophia put her finger to her lips. "He's sleeping," she whispered. "How are you?"

Kat nodded. "Rough day. I'll go, let him sleep."

"He's going to be out for hours. I'll buy you a coffee."

"It tastes like mud here."

Sophia smiled. "It has caffeine." She followed Kat out of the room. "Okay," she said in a normal voice. "What was so rough?"

"Found a girl beaten up this morning. Really bad. Just rode in the ambulance with her. She didn't look good."

"Did you know her?"

"I've seen her around. She worked at a restaurant nearby. She was beaten up and left behind the bins." Kat scowled. "I'd really like to catch up to the arsehole who did that and give him some back."

"I think I like you." Sophia glanced back in the room. "It's not far back to your office, right?"

"Five minute drive."

"Let me leave a note for him."

Kat looked at her watch. "Yeah, we need to head back. Terry and I are heading up to one of the locations Andy pinged. Beryl can keep you company."

Chapter Twenty

Vasily followed the bus. Ilya was keeping to the speed limit. He checked his dash. Just below the limit. Not too slow as to draw suspicion, and not over. Getting pulled over would be a messy disaster.

He checked the dash again, for the time. The drugs would be wearing off soon. Enough that some of the bigger girls would become a handful. The house was ten minutes away. He hadn't heard anything yet. He popped an earbud in and called his partner.

"Da?"

"It is me."

"I am having caller i.d. I know who it is. Why are you calling? We are almost there."

"No word from the boss yet. Something is not right."

"So call them, then. Not me. I have a lot on my hands."

"Okay. Fine." He punched the End button and called Jason. It rang a few times before it answered.

"The little Russian. Why are you calling me, mate? Lose the girls?"

"We are five minutes from house. I have not heard confirmation of our destination."

"Five minutes? Shit. You're early. I'm about thirty minutes out. Nobody's home, right now. Can you pull over somewhere and wait?"

"Their dope will run out soon. We need to get them under cover and drug them again."

"Fuck."

"Is there another destination close by?"

"No, no. That's the place." He paused. "Take the bus around the side and keep it out of sight. Keep the girls on the bus and keep them quiet. I'll be there as fast as I can. Don't screw up, okay?"

Vasily hung up the phone and called Ilya. "Keep going. I have instructions. Drive in and to the left of the house and get the bus out of sight of the road."

"Da."

Terry stopped on the side of the road and looked out the windscreen at the house in front of them. "We at the right place?"

Kat looked at the map on her phone. "It's where he pinged." She stared at the house too. "Doesn't look like any farm I've ever seen."

They were out past Kenthurst, in a neighbourhood of massive houses on really massive properties. In front of them was a spreading one-storey ranch style house that looked like it had three wings. It had a white wooden fence across the front of the property, with a gate almost dead centre. Terry reached behind him and grabbed his iPad out of the back seat and handed it to Kat. "I need to see around the back. Get this place up on maps, satellite view. It's humungous."

"What am I, your assistant?" She opened a maps app and let it centre on their location. She tapped the screen and switched to satellite mode. She held it over the centre console and they leaned together, looking at the screen.

A driveway, at least 300m long, led to what looked like a small traffic circle, with parking on either side large enough to handle half a dozen vehicles each.

"That's just stupid money," said Kat. "I think I want stupid money. That's nice."

Terry adjusted the screen, zooming to the many sections of roof. "No solar panels."

"No way. That'll never work."

He reached in front of her and popped open the glove box. He grabbed a handful of brochures, passed them to Kat and put the car in gear. "The gate's open. What's the worst that can happen?"

"Do you remember visiting Andy?"

They rolled past the open gate and toward the circle on the

driveway.

"This doesn't feel right. If this place had anything to do with human trafficking, there'd be security, right?"

"Maybe it's the wrong place," said Kat.

"So why did Andy ping here?"

"This is the place the locals had rumours about." Kat rolled down her window. Bell birds rang in the distance. Cicadas provided a continuous background level of noise. "That would drive me bonkers. City life is fine for me."

They reached the mini-traffic circle. "Left or right?"

Kat pointed left. Terry turned on his indicator and slowly took the corner.

"You used your turn signal? Jesus."

"Habits. This place is beautiful." He leaned forward and looked up at the roof. "Gorgeous."

Kat slapped his arm. "STOP."

Terry instinctively jammed his foot on the brake pedal, knocking his forehead on the steering wheel. "Ouch. What the hell?"

Kat had her hand over her mouth, batting at his arm. "Back up. Back up. Quietly."

A small bus was parked just around the corner of the house, out of sight of the road.

"Shit." Terry eased the car into reverse and backed until they couldn't see it.

"That's it, isn't it?" Kat pressed herself back in the seat, trying to physically get farther from the bus. "Get out of here before they see us."

"No. They're here." He rolled back to the circle and drove to the other side of the house. "They're here and we know it."

"I'll call the police."

"Call Beryl. She's already talking to the police." He opened the car door and winced as the hinges squealed against the rust. "Shit." He slowly pressed the door closed and leaned in the window. "Leave it running. If shit goes sideways, get the fuck out of here."

"Terry - "

He pointed at her and ran around the other side of the house. He passed by an open two car garage. He stopped. A Jeep Wrangler, with its top off, sat beside a Jaguar coupe. Keys for both hung on a hook on the wall. "Huh." He ducked around to the side and stopped again. There was a full-sized tennis court and an Olympic-sized swimming pool. "Jesus."

He stuck to the wall and crept toward a large window. "My fuck, this place is big." A courtyard the size of a small football field sat in the centre of a U-shape created by the three wings of the house. He heard, faintly, Russian accents. He'd gone around almost three-quarters of the building. The two voices were louder. He took out his phone and started recording video and eased around the final corner. The bus was parked and idling. Two men were sitting on the front bumper of the bus having a smoke, one wiry, scary looking guy and one who looked like a monster.

He stepped carefully over the gravel and raised his phone to record through the back window of the bus. He stepped up on the back bumper to see inside. The bus rocked and he heard the Russians yell something. "Oh, fuck."

He scrambled back around the corner of the house and handed his phone to Kat. "Watch this," he whispered. "Mute the volume."

Vasily looked at his watch. "I am not doing anything with these girls until the muscles show up. Call them, Ilya. Find out what's taking them so long."

He waited. He paced the gravel in front of the bus, arms crossed while Ilya dialled. He didn't like talking to Jason. The guy freaked him out. He watched his partner on the phone, gesticulating and swearing in Russian. He waited until the big guy was finished. Ilya made like he was going to throw the phone, then checked himself.

"I think maybe you talk to him next time, Vasily. I hate that man's arrogance."

"Is he coming?"

"Da. He and the woman. They said they're close. Whatever 'close' means. We should get started."

Vasily shook his head. "Twenty-two of them and two of us. Even drugged, if they start taking off we will never be able to contain them."

"They are little girls."

"That is a million dollars in that bus. Do not fuck around with a million dollars."

Terry and Kat had retreated behind a brick wall separating the front yard from the barbecue area. Kat watched the video a third time. It was a jumpy pan of the girls in the bus, from behind, looking worse for wear. Their clothes looked dirty, and their hair greasy. She pointed at one girl, sitting with her head turned slightly left, her shoulder length black hair tucked behind her ear. "Do you think?"

"Andy's daughter? Maybe. Hard to tell. This is no church group."

"What are we going to do?"

Terry puffed out his cheeks and blew out a breath. "Well, we can't take out those two Russians."

He popped his head around the corner of the house quickly, then pulled it back. "They aren't in front of the bus any more. Probably our only chance. I'll get in and escort them out."

"Dumb idea, Ter."

"We've got to get them out of there."

"I'm going in to usher them out. You stay at the door and get them clear. We need to get them into the bush before the Russians know we're gone."

"I should go in. It's more dangerous."

"Your chivalry is blocking your brain. It's twenty-two young girls being trafficked for god knows what and you think another man going in the bus is going to help move things along? You'll start a panic."

Terry nodded. "That makes sense. But I don't like it."

They ran to the back of the bus. The door with a window in the top half was locked.

Kat muttered something under breath and moved to the side of the bus. They were on the lee side, blocked from view from the house. "How do you open the door?"

Terry reached under the footstep and pushed a button. The door sprung open a crack and he pulled it the rest of the way. He looked to his left. A stand of pine trees separated the yard from the surrounding bush, and beyond that, the next property. "We get them to the trees fast, first. Then sort out what to do next."

Kat stood looking into the bus. The key was in the ignition. "Why don't we just drive them out of here?"

"We'd be sitting ducks. They'd catch us in minutes."

"Shit. Okay. Get ready."

She stepped into the bus in a crouch, trying to keep her head below the window line. Up close the girls looked younger than she had thought them to be. "Fucking arseholes."

"Who are you?"

Kat lifted her finger and put it to her lips. "Whisper. A friend and I are here to get all of you out of here. Are you Kelly?"

"I said *who are you*?"

"My name is Kat. I work with your dad, Andy. Andy's your father, right? We've been looking for you. Did you leave the message in the closet in the house?"

"Yes, I am Kelly," she whispered. She broke into a huge smile. "You found my message." Then she frowned again. "The girls are drugged. They shuffle like old school zombies. This will never work."

Kat peered out the window, then squatted again aside Kelly.

"Why aren't you drugged?"

"I am some. I figured out what was going on just after I was grabbed. Made myself throw up every chance I got. I would have left, except for the other girls. I couldn't get any of them to do the same thing." There were tears in her eyes. "I really tried. I did."

"That's okay. We'll do what we can. You first. Stay low." Kat held out her hand. Kelly looked at her, and her hand, for a minute, then took it and slid out of the bus seat, crouched, and waddled to the front of the bus.

"The guy out there is named Terry. He's okay. Listen to what he says."

"You trust him?"

Kat rolled her eyes. "He's as good as men get. Better than the two driving you around. Hustle."

She crammed herself by the front seat of the bus and let Kelly pass. She waited until Terry took her hand and moved her to the side of the bus, then looked back at the rest of the girls. Kelly was not wrong. They all looked drugged.

She kept crouched and shuffled to the back of the bus, tapped each of the girls on the legs or arms all the way to the back, with no response. There were two seats on the left of the aisle and one on the right until she got to the back. A bench of four seats spanned the width of the bus. There was a gap about a metre wide between the bench seats and the back door of the bus.

She squatted in front of the girl on the back bench facing the open aisle. She'd be the easiest extraction. "Hey, sweetie, are you awake?"

The girl looked pre-pubescent. Her eyes were open, but glassy. She sniffed and tried to focus. She mumbled something in a language Kat didn't understand.

"Shit." She took the girl's hands and tried to get her to her feet. "Come on."

The girls arms were slack.

"Jesus, let's go."

Terry and Kelly squatted beside the bus door, waiting. "I'm going to need you to help us, Kelly. When Kat gets the other girls out, I'm going to need you to help get them together and get them to those trees." He pointed. "And then we're getting the hell out of here."

Kelly shook her head. "Most of the girls are out of it. It's not going to work."

"Think positive, kid."

"You sound like my dad."

Terry smiled. "So stay beside the bus and keep the girls calm as they come out."

"Okay, but I'm just saying."

Terry leaned in the door to check on Kat's progress. She was at the back of the bus, trying to get one of the girls moving.

She was having no luck.

He pulled back and leaned against the bus. "Damn. This is taking too long."

"Why are you here and not my dad?"

"I'll explain everything once we get out of here."

"Is he okay?"

"He's fine." He leaned his head back into the bus. "Come on, Kat, this is taking too long."

Kat shook a third girl. She had drool on her chin and a glassy look in her eyes. "Come on. Dammit. This isn't working." She slapped the girl, gently, on the face, and the girl's head lolled to one side. Kat caught movement out of her peripheral vision and ducked to a squat. She slowly raised herself above the window line and watched the two Russians slowly walking toward the bus, arguing with each other.

She shifted to the other side of the bus and leaned over two of the girls. She prised open a window and reached a hand out and tapped the side of the bus. "Hey, guys," she whispered. "Get out of here. The Russians are coming."

"Get out of the bus."

"I'm not going to have time. Get Kelly out of here. I'll figure something out."

"No way!"

Kat looked over her shoulder ducked down, waving them away and she disappeared.

Terry stood looking at the bus. "No."

Kelly grabbed his arm. "If you guys work with my dad, you're capable. She will be okay. We need to go or Vasily and Ilya are going to catch us and you're no match Vasily, the skinny one, let alone both of them."

Terry shook his head. "Can't leave Kat."

"I'm gone." Kelly started running toward the trees.

Terry stood, hands out, looking at Kelly's receding figure. He looked back at the bus, and Kat, then ran to the back as the Russian voices got louder. He squatted down and peered around the corner.

"Where are they?" asked Ilya.

"They said five more minutes." Vasily slid his phone in his pocket. "Probably safe to move them. One at a time into the house."

They stopped at the partially opened bus door. "What is this?" Vasily pulled the door all the way open.

"Did they get out?"

He shook his head as he took a quick glance at the girls in the bus. "Someone tried." He looked at the door again.

He got out of the bus and pushed the door closed. He looked around. "Call them. Find out how far away they are. We need more people."

Ilya pressed redial on his phone and stepped to the front of the bus. "Where are you?"

Terry backed away, keeping the bus between him and the Russians. He hammered out a text on his phone.

Dan, in trouble at the house Andy pinged in the Hills district. How fast can you get here? Then he sent him his location.

Kate was behind the back seat, up against the back door, gesturing through the small window for him to get out of there. Then she ducked down out of sight again.

"Jesus, Kat," muttered Terry. He checked over his shoulder. Kelly had disappeared into the bush. He moved back closer to the bus and squatted again, peering around the corner.

Kat's face peered out of the back door window.

Terry slumped back. "Oh, man. This is bad."

Chapter Twenty-One

Ilya had his back to Terry. He closed his phone and turned to Vasily. "We are to get out of here. Take the girls to the other place. They will be here in a minute to help."

"Help? We do not need their fucking help to drive a bus."

"He was pissed we let someone find us. We should not piss him off more."

"Fuck him."

Terry ducked back out of the way as Vasily wrenched the door open.

"I will drive. You follow."

Terry tried the back door handle again. It was still locked. "Shit, Kat." The pitched whine of a large truck down shifting drew his attention to the road. A ute rapidly decelerated and turned into the driveway. Help had arrived. Help for the Russians. It was the same ute that dropped Andy off behind the office.

The bus lurched as it started, a black ball of smoke belched from the tailpipe. Terry back-pedalled and ran for the bush. He got behind a stand of pines and squatted, watching the bus trundle up the driveway to the ute that was blocking its path. Ilya followed in a comically small Corolla. Vasily jumped out of the bus and approached the ute. Terry couldn't make out the words, but the volume increased loud enough to hear the yelling from the guy in the ute. He stepped out. The guy who threw Andy to the parking lot. Jason.

"My money is on muscles."

Terry jumped and fell backwards, ricocheting off a pine trunk. "Jesus Christ, you scared the shit out of me."

Kelly pointed at the bus. "Your friend, Kat, she's still in the bus, right?"

Terry dusted leaves off his arse. "Yes. They didn't notice you were missing."

"We've got to get her out. If they find her, they aren't going to be nice." She grabbed Terry by the arm. "Oh, no. Look."

Jason pushed Vasily to one side and stepped into the bus. A woman got out of the passenger side of the ute and followed him. As she got to the door, Jason leaned out of the bus, pointed at Vasily and yelled something.

The Russian ran onto the bus, and a couple of seconds later ran down the steps and scanned the edge of the property. He locked onto the pines, looking directly at Kelly and Terry.

"Now they've noticed."

"They can see us."

"No. Stay still, stay low, and stay quiet. Vasily is only guessing where we went."

Jason shoved Vasily against the bus and slapped his face. Ilya jumped out of the car and tried to help his friend, but was blocked by Rhonda. He tried to push her out of the way and she grabbed his hand, locked his wrist and had him face-first on the driveway before Terry had a chance to blink. "Damn."

"That escalated quickly." Kelly tried to make herself smaller.

Jason got back on the bus and closed the door. The woman got in the driver's seat of the ute and the vehicle turned, leaving furrows in the green lawn as she did.

Terry took his phone out again.

Dan, the bus with the girls has left. Kat is on the bus. It is following the ute that dropped Andy off at the office. These are mean fuckers.

"What now?"

"Now we get the hell out of here, before the Russians find us."

"How far to where my father is?"

"Over an hour's drive. We need to get my car. It's on the other side."

"What about Kat?"

Terry watched the Russians discussing something. "She's smart.

She'll figure out a way. Can you drive?"

"I don't have a licence."

"Didn't ask that."

Terry dug the key fob out of his pocket and handed it to her.

"What's the plan?"

Terry took a deep breath. "I'm going to draw them away. I'm going to go farther down the tree line, then pop out and get their attention. Wait until they're well past you then go for the car. I think I can out run them. I definitely can't out fight them."

Kelly squinted at Terry. "If they catch you, you'll end up smashed."

"So they better not catch me. Stay here until you see them start moving. Okay?"

Kelly nodded, and chewed a nail. "You sure I can do this?"

"You're Andy's daughter," smiled Terry. "You definitely can."

Andy walked slowly between Sophia and Beryl to the cafeteria on the ground floor of the hospital. "You both are shadowing me like you think I'll fall over. I'm good."

Beryl snorted. "I could knock you over with a light slap to the back of your head."

Sophia laughed.

"Watch it, wifey. I'll take guff from the old woman, but you need to respect your elders."

"Watch yourself, kid."

Andy smiled and turned to say something to Beryl, wincing as he put pressure on his ribs. "Nice to see you back to your normal self."

"I'm always my normal self."

"Nah. You've been more motherly than usual. Not the 'crack your knuckles with a wooden spoon' mother we all know and love, but a coddling, overly solicitous and frankly, unsettling mother. Glad to have the old you back." He smiled. "Emphasis on - "

"Say 'old' and I'll put you back in that hospital bed."

"I'm getting out tomorrow. You wouldn't dare."

They took a table in the corner of the cafeteria. "You two stay here and I'll get food," said Sophia. "My treat. What do you want?"

"Anything fried," said Andy. "I'm getting too healthy in here."

"Nothing for me, dear." Beryl tapped Andy on the arm. "This might be a good time to make a life change. Get healthy."

Sophia chuckled. "Good luck. I'll be back in a minute."

Andy nodded thanks. "Beryl, This is not a good time. I'm already fighting to find my daughter. Jokes aside, I need to get out of here and get back in the mix." He held up his hands. "I know. I'll do as the good doctor says. One more night in here. But that's it."

"Tell me about her."

Andy took a deep breath. "Spitting image of her mother," he pointed at himself, "despite the corrupted blood in her system." He smiled. "Really smart. Gets that from her mother, too."

Sophia returned with a tray, putting a chicken parm and chips in front of Andy and a chicken Caesar in front of Beryl. She put a club sandwich at her own place and put the tray on an empty table beside them.

"I didn't need anything."

Sophia raised her eyebrows. "Andy was right. You're old, and possibly forgetful." She laughed as she dodged Beryl's swing.

"No respect." Beryl picked up a fork and stabbed a piece of chicken. "Thanks. I actually am kind of hungry." She nodded at Andy. "Dig in, kiddo. You need the energy to heal."

They ate, mostly in silence. Andy finished up the chicken parm and was wiping up the remaining tomato sauce with his fries when Beryl cleared her throat. "Look, you guys. I'm going to check on the girl Kat brought in, see how she's doing. I'll meet you back in Andy's room when I'm done."

Sophia picked at the remnants of her sandwich. "We should go with you."

"Yeah, I could use more of a break from that hospital bed. What girl did Kat bring in?"

"She was behind that new chicken place. Really beaten up bad. Kat called the ambulance and rode in with her." She wiped her mouth with a paper napkin and stood. "No identification on her. I think she's still a Jane Doe."

Sophia and Andy also stood. "You know the room she's in?" asked Andy.

"Yeah."

It was a double room. The girl was closest to the window. A middle-aged woman on a respirator was in the bed near the door. She followed them in with her eyes.

The young girl was barely conscious. She saw Sophia first, and frowned. "No. No. *Tow chhngay.*"

"It's okay. We're not going to hurt you."

Andy leaned forward. *"Yeung nung chuoy anak."*

Beryl rested her hand on the bed. "What did you say, Andy? What did she say?"

"She told us to go away. I told her we were here to help her."

"She's petrified," said Beryl.

"You're not kidding." Sophia smiled at the girl and tried to hold her hand. She pulled back.

Andy asked her another question, then listened to the answer. Sophia interjected with a question. They went back and forth a couple of times. They both bowed to her. *"Arkoun Chraen."*

He turned to Beryl and Sophia. "We should leave. Beryl, can you reach everyone? We need to talk."

Chapter Twenty-Two

Stew and Dan walked into Mac Durridge's office. It was small, but functional. Mac was sitting behind an old wooden desk doing something on a computer.

"How's it going, mate?" asked Stew.

Mac pushed his chair back and stood.

"You're back." Mac held out his hand across the desk. "You must be Dan."

"I am. Have you found out anything?"

"Not really enough time. What are you driving?"

"My Mazda,' said Stew. "Where are we going?"

"I've checked out the place you told me about." He shook his head. "Beautiful house." He came around the desk and ushered them out. "Got to take your wheels. I've only got a two-seater."

"And you don't want to pay for the petrol."

"Seriously, mate. Two-seater. Which one of you wants to stay behind?"

Dan and Stew walked down the stairs while Mac locked up. "You serious about this guy? Seems like a flake."

"He's okay. He's got a good track record. A little unconventional, and a one-man show, but he's the best I know up here."

Mac trotted down the stairs and caught up to them. "Talking about me? I'm a small shop, Dan, but I'm good. Very good."

"That's what he told me. How far away are we going?"

"Ten minutes east of here." He scanned the parking lot behind the office. "That blue one?"

"The same one I drove less than a week ago." Stew pushed the key fob. "You sit up front and give directions."

"I'll stick the address in your bloody GPS. Dan can sit up front."

"That's okay I need to stretch my legs."

Mac shrugged and got in the front passenger side. Stew started the car and Mac entered the address in the dashboard GPS.

Dan looked between the seats. "Thirteen minutes."

"Yeah," said Mac.

"You said ten."

Stew smiled. "We can do it in ten."

It took eleven.

"Slow up. Just ahead on the right. Pull over across the street." Mac tapped on the dashboard and scanned the area. "Look out for a white ute with a Roo bar on the front."

Dan scratched his chin. "We've seen pictures of it."

"The guy looks hard and the woman he runs with looks harder," said Mac. "Not looking to run into them again."

Dan looked at Mac with new respect. "You tangled with them? You came out of it better than Stew and Andy."

Mac held up his hands. "Oh, hell no. I'm smarter than both of you guys. They didn't get a chance." He nodded. "Look at that place."

The house across from which they were conspicuously stopped looked like a giant had absentmindedly scattered a dozen large concrete blocks. At its tallest the place was three stories tall. A two hundred metre drive pushed the house off the street leading up to, on the right, two blocks side by side making a four car garage, two either side of a centre wall.

The left side of the house was fronted by a large, well-manicured lawn. A spur off the drive led to a circular area in front of the main doors, with a portico stretching out far enough to provide foul weather cover to passengers entering or leaving the house.

The gate at the street end of the drive was closed, made of the same wrought iron fencing circling the house. A speaker and keypad was mounted near the gate.

Dan pointed. "Cameras on the corner posts of the fencing, and on top of the left gate post. We aren't walking in there unnoticed."

"What are we supposed to be looking for?"

Stew looked in the rear-view mirror at Dan who nodded. "We believe there's a busload of twenty or so girls on its way. Human trafficking. They're probably for sale."

"Jesus, man. Call the cops. The Feds."

"Yeah, talked to the cops. Not getting the kind of support we need."

"No actionable proof?"

"Yeah. Let's sit here for a while, if you don't mind," said Stew. "Maybe something will happen."

"And you can tell me what gut checks got you both up here."

Dan's phone chimed. "Hang on a sec. Message from Terry." He was midway through reading it when his phone chimed again. "And one from Beryl."

He showed the address to Stew. "Get here. Fast. Terry has run into trouble." He waited until the navigation system had plotted a route, then made a call. Put the phone on speaker. "Beryl, you've got me, Stew and Mac, the guy from the Central Coast. What's going on? Is Andy okay?"

"I'm fine, Dan. How far out are you?"

"To be determined. Terry's in trouble. We're about half an hour out from there." Dan nudged Stew from the back seat. "Quicker if the driver gets the lead out. What's so urgent?"

"Put me on speaker."

"You are."

"We are here too. We're in the hospital, so we can't talk too loud. I was just introduced to the girl Kat rescued the other morning. She's going to be okay, but she's freaking out. Someone at that restaurant tried to kill her. She got away and hid under the cardboard waste where Kat found her the next morning. She was trafficked, Dan, from Cambodia. Came in almost a month ago. She told us that she was sold to the chicken guy. He prostitutes her out at night, when she isn't cleaning tables. This is right here in our town."

"Call Wazza and that Ryan guy. Get it in front of them."

There was a pause on the line.

"You there?" asked Dan.

"I am. She said that there were police involved somehow. She was told that if she went to the police she'd disappear. Nobody could help her."

Dan slid in the back seat as Stew took an aggressive corner. "What's her name?"

"Mony Sok. She's petrified. She hasn't told the hospital who she is because she's afraid she'll get sent back to where she escaped from."

Dan rubbed his face. "Jesus. Fine mess we're getting ourselves into. Is she safe now?"

"Yeah."

"Hey," yelled Stew. "Tell Jane I said the girl needs to be protected. I'll sort it out when we're back in town."

"You catch that?"

"Yeah," said Andy. "The whole fucking ward heard him. I'll let her know. When are you back?"

"Five, six hours, if we're lucky."

Andy nodded. "See you then." He hung up. "Anyone know if Dr

Jane is in the house?"

"You look like death warmed over, dear. You head back to your room. I'll find Jane."

"Give me a break. I'll be fine, Sophia."

"You know better than to cross mama bear."

"Damn straight, hun." Beryl marched off looking for Dr Jane.

"Do you think this is connected to, to our daughter?"

Andy shook his head. "Not directly. A month ago Kelly was home. Maybe the same arseholes, though." He winced as he turned a corner in the hall toward his room. "God damned ribs. I'm here. You can go. Track down Beryl and make sure Jane keeps an eye on the girl."

"Mony."

"Yeah. Mony."

Sophia gave him a kiss. "I will. You rest. I want you out of here. Soon."

Chapter Twenty-Three

Terry moved quickly through the bush. He didn't want them to start looking for Kelly yet. He needed them completely focussed on him.

He got near the back of the house and stumble onto the lawn. They were on the other side of the yard. "You fucking Russians are so stupid" he yelled. "Wow. I got the girl."

The stopped yelling at each other and turned, looking for him. He stepped farther on to the lawn, toward the back of the house, and raised both middle fingers.

Vasily pulled a hand gun from the back of his jeans and pointed it at Terry. "Come over to me." He pulled the hammer back. "Or I shoot you."

Terry looked at the distance, and the gun. It looked like a .32

Glock and he was at least 200 metres away. The odds of getting hit at that range were very small. And he needed them to chase him. He sprinted toward the back of the house. Two shots echoed against the trees. "If I heard it, it didn't hit me," muttered Terry as he ran. He was out of their sight now, so he had no idea if they were chasing him, or if Kelly was doing her part. He had to trust her.

The chasing question was answered almost immediately. A shard of brick from the house flew into the side of his face as he heard the shot. "Shit. Too close." He ducked and ran, getting to the corner before another shot rang out.

He was 20 metres from where his car was parked. Almost there.

Except it was missing.

He stopped. "Kelly?"

A Russian accented voice spoke behind him. "I would shoot you now, except I need to find the girl. Turn around."

Terry did as he was told. Vasily stood at the corner of the house, his handgun pointed at Terry's centre mass, unwavering.

"So, where is she?"

Terry shrugged. "What are you talking about?"

"I can hurt you in ways you wished you were still dead. I will hurt you until you tell me, then I will hurt you more. Where. Is. The. Girl?"

"Dude, so, like that first sentence made absolutely no sense, and I was just fucking with the bus. Pretty girls in there, but I like them older. I'm not a creep. Are you a creep? What's your name? I'm Terry."

"Terry. A pussy name."

"Like Vasily is any better."

"Where is the girl?" He shot the ground in front of Terry's feet, gravel spraying into his legs. He took a couple of steps closer. "You are too close to me for to run away. I will not miss at this distance."

Terry sniffed. He had to keep stalling until Kelly got out of there. "Another couple of minutes."

"What?"

"Another couple and I'll tell you."

Vasily raised the gun and held it with two hands. "Your shoulder, I think."

Terry heard the accelerating car. Vasily looked to his right in surprise as Terry's car roared toward him. He dove sideways, rolling and slamming into the garage wall. He gun flew another 20 metres away.

Kelly pulled up beside Terry. "Need a lift? Your face is bleeding. You okay?"

Terry scrambled into the passenger seat. "Go, go, go. Where's the big one?"

"Put your seatbelt on. This thing rides like shit." Kelly floored the accelerator, resulting in more noise than speed. "This is yours?" She continued the pressure on the accelerator, churning across the lawn.

Terry struggled with the belt as Kelly manoeuvred onto the drive. There was a sharp crack as a bullet buried itself in the back, left fender. "Faster, Kelly."

"Not even a 'thanks'? I rescued you."

Terry looked out the back of the car. Ilya was hobbling toward Vasily, holding his right arm close to his chest. Vasily was sitting on the ground, one hand on a leg and the other pointing his Glock at the car. "So, faster, and what did you do to the big one?"

Kelly grimace. "Feel kinda bad about that one. I sucker punched him with your car. There's a ding on the fender. He's tough, though. I don't think I broke anything."

Terry watched her accelerate onto the road from the driveway. "So you can drive."

"You should never assume people can't do things. Where do we go from here?"

Dan pointed ahead at the house, about 500 metres away. "There. Andy pinged just in front of this place." They watched Terry's car leave the Hills house and accelerate away from them. Dan stopped at the head of the drive. "I think they beat us here."

Stew leaned forward between the seats and pointed to Dan's right. "We should leave. That guy has a gun."

Mac pulled up his trouser leg and removed a revolver from an ankle holster. "So do I."

Dan put the car into gear and slowly drove away. "We're not getting into a gunfight. Call Terry. Find out what's going on. See if he's found Kat yet." His phone started ringing. "Never mind." He tossed it to Mac. "Put it on speaker."

"What's up, kid?"

"Who's this? Where's Dan."

"Right here," said Dan. "Where are you?"

"We just left the house. Track my phone."

"We saw you leave. Kat with you?"

"No, but Kelly is. Kelly, pull over. I'll drive."

"Kelly is driving? She's - "

"Thirteen. Yeah. Forget it. Don't track my phone. Track Kat's. She's hidden on the bus with twenty-one other girls. Sex trafficking. There's an auction. Was supposed to be today at that house, Kelly thinks, but now it's moved somewhere else. Maybe different night, too. You track Kat's phone and I'll track Kat's phone and we should catch up with each other soon."

Dan watched Terry's car pull into a service station and park by the air hose. A willowy girl jumped out of the driver's seat and switched places with Terry, his phone plastered to his bloody face.

"We're right behind you. Hold up." Dan pulled the car to a stop beside Terry. The car was covered in dirt. Terry had dried blood on one side of his face. His head was back on the headrest, eyes closed. A young girl sat in the passenger seat, a bundle of nerves. "You're Andy's daughter."

Terry opened his eyes. "Kelly, this is Dan, the boss. The big guy behind him is Stew and the other guy is, I think, Mac. Not one of ours, but still a good guy, I'm told."

"Stew, find some food and something to drink for Kelly," said Dan. "Kelly, after you eat, I want you to go with Terry and Mac back to Mac's place so we can drop him off, then Terry will drive you back to Campbelltown to see your father. Stew and I are going to find Kat."

Kelly looked at Mac. "Is your place closer to where my father is than here, or farther?"

"Farther."

She shook her head. "No way. I need to see my father."

Dan took a deep breath and was about to argue against that idea when Mac interjected. "Absolutely. We'll take you to Campbelltown. We can worry about me getting home later. Not a big deal."

She nodded. "Thanks."

Stew arrived with a bag full of junk food. "Take this. Something for everyone. We're following Kat."

Kat winced and tried to adjust herself. The space behind the backseat was barely large enough for a couple of suitcases. She was cramping up and every time the bus went over a bounce she had to clench her teeth to keep the pain from turning into noise.

She knew Terry and Dan and probably Stew were tracking her phone. As long as she stayed out of sight she would be okay.

As long as she stayed out of sight.

She looked at her phone, slowly and quietly tapping it in her hand. She looked up at the door latch. She'd unlocked it, but wasn't keen on jumping out while they were moving. And she really wasn't interested in leaving the girls behind.

But she saw the guy who was driving the bus, and there was no way she could hold her own against him.

She looked once more at her phone and slid it into a pocket on the door, screen facing in. She waited for the chance.

Dan sat with one hand on the steering wheel and the other on the gearshift knob. "We getting close?"

Stew had his phone open to the tracking app. A blue dot pulsated on the screen. "We're about a klick behind. Staying steady." He looked up at the road, as if he could see the bus. "Go faster. If Kat is hurt, I'm going to get a workout."

Dan nodded and pressed on the accelerator. "This thing handles like a pig. Any idea where they're going?"

"No. Nowhere Andy pinged, that's for sure."

Dan pressed the accelerator harder. The car got louder, but not much faster. "Piece of shit."

Stew leaned forward. "Hang on. I think it's stopped." He manipulated the screen and magnified the map around the dot. "At a servo. Ahead on the left, past the next set of lights."

The bus slowed and turned off the road. Kat braced herself against the bumps. The girls were starting to make some noise, speaking to each other in a language she couldn't understand.

"Shut up back there," bellowed the man behind the wheel. "Shut. Up."

They all stopped. Even if they didn't understand a word he said, they understood the tone.

The bus engine stopped and the bus rocked as the driver stepped out. Kat rested her hand on the back door handle. She waited a second, held her breath and turned it, and grimaced as it squealed. She took another breath and leaned into the door.

And stopped when she heard footsteps walk past.

"Fucking hell," said the voice. "Where's the bloody tank?"

Kat leaned her ear against the door. She'd wait. He had to go in the station to pay.

"Hey, it's me. Jason." He was on the phone. "This is a massive cluster fuck, mate. I'm putting fuel in the bus. You owe me." He listened. "No. One of them is missing. No, I don't know which one, I didn't ask their fucking names. And I'm not a fucking babysitter. If it wasn't for the money we're getting for these bitches I'd leave them here."

Kat gripped the door handle. She heard the pump trigger clunk when the tank had filled.

"Jesus, man. You're going to owe me over a hundred dollars for fuel. Why am *I* driving? Because somehow your hot shot Russians lost control of the situation. Tell Prescott he's going to pay for this."

Kat heard Jason holster the pump and his boots echo off the pavement as he headed in to pay. She looked over the back seat at the girls one last time and opened the back door.

Stew pointed at the bus. "There. Kat's getting out of the back. Go."

Kat was running toward the road when Dan pulled to a stop. He leaned out the window of the car. "Kat! Over here."

She spun in her tracks. "Dan. Shit. Someone needs to drive the bus. The girls are in there."

Stew jumped out. "I'll follow you guys. Go."

Kat jumped into the seat Stew had vacated. "What took you guys so long?"

"Glad you're okay."

Kat nodded toward the bus. "It's going to get ugly." Jason had left the servo and was walking back to the bus, spinning the ring of keys on his index finger.

Dan accelerated and got to the front of the bus before Jason did. The door was open and Stew was reaching under the dash, trying to get at the wiring harness. "Stew. Move it. Another time."

Jason noticed them. He pulled the handgun from the small of his back and held it down by his side. "What's going on, guys?" He looked at Kat and Dan, then leaned into the bus. He raised the gun and pointed it in the door. "You're going to want to get out of there. Now."

Stew's eyes narrowed. "You."

"I owe you a beating."

Stew stood and looked at the girls. They stared back at him, half-doped, not comprehending what was going on. "We're going to have a discussion about that." He looked at the handgun. "Some day when you're man enough to come at me without that crutch."

"Get out before I blow a hole in your kneecap."

Stew held up his hands and walked out of the bus. "Another day, shit stain."

Jason watched him as he got in the car. He held his gun part of the way away from his leg and he backed into the bus. "You don't want to run into me again, trust me, mate. Follow me and I'll kill the girls, one at a time."

He pulled the door shut and the bus started and rolled out of the service station.

"You think he was bluffing? About shooting the girls?" asked Dan.

"Don't risk it," said Kat. "I left my phone hidden on the bus. Battery should be good for at least twelve hours. We'll find them. Where's Kelly?"

Chapter Twenty-Four

Kelly fussed with her seatbelt. "How far away are we?"

Mac eased off the highway to the offramp to Campbelltown Road. "Fifteen minutes. Terry, call Beryl and tell her to get Kelly's mother to the office."

"My mother? My mother came here?" Tears welled up in her eyes.

Mac looked at Terry. "You haven't told her yet? Wow. Yes. I haven't met her yet, but I hear she's a rocket."

"She's going to kill me."

"I don't think so."

"I stink. I need a shower."

Beryl hung up her phone and hugged Sophia. She pulled back at the stiff response and laughed. "That was Terry. He's about fifteen minutes away. With Kelly."

Sophia looked at her, stunned. "My Kaliyanei? You found her already?" She covered her face with her hands and cried. "Thank you so much."

Beryl pulled her back in for another hug. "It's what we do. But knowing the boys, it's just the tip of the iceberg." She pulled back and looked at her. "You better clean up. Don't want your daughter seeing her mother in such a state."

Sophia wiped away tears. "She's going to want to see her father, too."

"And she will."

The door at the bottom of the stairs opened and quick feet raced up the stairs. The door pushed open and Kelly burst through and jumped at her mother.

Beryl, Terry and Mac stood back, giving them space.

"Where are the others?" asked Beryl.

"They're tracking the bus with the girls," said Terry. "I was talking to them about an hour ago. They were heading back up toward Mac's stomping grounds."

"I should have swapped places with Kat," said Mac.

"Never would have happened. She's committed." Terry looked at the time on his phone. "We need to get the cops involved. Think Kelly will be okay to tell her story?"

Beryl shook her head. "Give her a little bit of space. And she needs to see her father." Beryl placed her hands on the mother's and daughter's shoulders. "Let's go see dad."

Andy was slipping in and out of sleep, his body using most of its energy for healing. Permanently tired. The walking earlier had drained him. His eyes were closed and he was visualising what he was going to do to the big Limey bastard when he saw him again when he heard footsteps come into his room. He took a deep breath, pushing through the pain in his ribs. "You just checked my blood pressure."

"Hi dad," said Kelly.

His eyes snapped open and he sat upright, gritting his teeth. Sweat beaded on his forehead as he fought though the pain. He held his arms open and Kelly melted into them.

She leaned her chin on his shoulder. "Are you okay?"

He leaned back and looked at his daughter through tears. "Fantastic, now. How?"

"Kat and Terry and a couple of others found me and got me out of the bus I was in." She smiled, shyly. "I drove Terry's car." Her smile melted away as fast as it appeared. "There are others. In the bus. We need to find them."

Andy pushed the call button repeatedly, He swung his feet to the floor and looked at Sophia and Beryl. "Ladies, I'm going to get dressed. Step back and pull the curtain, will you, Beryl. Unless you want an eyeful."

The nurse came in, a young Asian guy with "Toby" on the name tag on his chest. "What are you doing, Mr Smith?"

"Hey, Toby. I'm getting the fuck out of here with my daughter and wife. Get this cannula out my hand, will you? Better you, than have me tear something."

Toby grabbed the chart off the end of the bed and flipped through the last couple of pages. "Doc says you should be in here a couple more days."

"Jane says it's okay."

"I seriously doubt that."

"She'll say it's okay. Look, I feel fantastic." He stood and took off his gown, holding eye contact with the nurse. He winked and grabbed his clothes out of the drawer in the table beside his bed. "I'm going, mate. I'll sign whatever waiver I have to sign, but I'm going." He pulled on a pair of boxers and his shorts. Slipped his T-shirt on and held out his hand. "Cannula?"

Toby dropped the chart on the bed and shook his head. He peeled the tape back, pulled out the needle and held a cotton ball over the spot of blood. "You'll need a plaster."

"That's the least of my problems, pal." Andy loaded his pockets with wallet and keys and picked up his shoes. "Show me what I have to sign." He pulled the curtain back. "Let's get the hell out of here, ladies."

Andy stepped out of the hospital with Sophia on one arm and Kelly on the other. He stopped and inhaled a deep breath through his nose.

The pain pills kept the ribs at bay. "Great to be outside again. What are we driving?"

"Mine," said Beryl." She waggled a finger at Andy before he had a chance to speak. "And you're not driving. I will. You'll sit up front with me. Kelly and Sophia sit in the back."

Andy dropped the sheets of paper waiving all liability against the hospital for being such a stupid person to discharge themselves before the doc said it was okay on the floor. He eased slowly into the seat, his bipartite patella causing him some pain when he bent his leg. His ribs edged through the pain medicine. "Son of a bitch. I don't think I can get out."

"Worry about that later," said Beryl.

"It's a five fucking minute drive to the office, Beryl. Later is not that much later."

Sophia smacked him on the shoulder from the center spot of the back seat, then realised what she had done when he winced. "Language. Oh I'm so sorry are you okay?"

He reached back and put his hand on top of hers on his shoulder. "I'm fine. I'm better than fine. The pain reminds me I'm still alive. I'm getting better every minute."

Beryl started the car and Andy adjusted the rear-view mirror to see his wife. "Thank you for coming."

She had a half smile on her face. "I didn't come for you, husband. I came for our daughter. And now that I've found her, maybe I should go back home."

Andy looked at his wife. "Beryl, the airport, please. The wench wants to go home."

She looked at him and back at Sophia. "You two are made for each other. We'll be back at the office in a couple of minutes. Don't get too comfortable."

Chapter Twenty-Five

Terry walked into the office with two large pizzas.

Dan pointed at the conference room and grabbed four beers from the kitchen fridge. "Extra cheese? Better have extra cheese."

"Just bring the beer, boss."

Dan chuckled and followed him into the conference room. He flipped the lid on the first box, pushed it to one side and grabbed a slice from the other and dropped it on a paper plate. "We're stuck." He twisted the top off the bottle. "Running in circles. Lost the signal on Kat's phone ten minutes after the bus was out of our sight."

"Where's Andy? And Beryl?" Terry leaned back and looked out the conference room door. "Shouldn't they be here?"

"Andy is reuniting with his family." Dan looked at his watch.

"And Beryl is probably queueing up another episode of Murder She Wrote. The relief at finding Kelly has drained her. She needs a break. This is just us spit balling. We need ideas. We almost had them. We've got to find those girls."

Terry struggled to twist the top off his beer, pulling it back as Kat reached for it to help. "No, I've got it." He opened it, tossed the cap in her general direction and took a swig. "We need to dig through the dark web deeper. Might get some federal attention. You think you can let them know what we're doing so I don't end up in Long Bay?"

Stew grunted. "Might make a man out of you."

Kat choked on her beer. "Seriously, though. Terry and I have a score to settle." She grabbed a slice. "What's the next step?"

Dan held up his hand. "Quiet."

Jason drove.

Rhonda had the McGinnis Investigations website open on her phone to the "About Us" page. She was looking at Terry's face. "We there?"

"Same place I dropped off that other guy."

"Where are they now, though? We need to find them, and get them to tell us where the girl is."

Jason braked to a stop in the back parking lot. He pointed to windows on the third floor. "Lights are on. Somebody's home. Shall we pay them a visit?"

Dan flicked on the TV in the conference room and pulled up the security feed. Jason's truck was stopped in the middle of the lot. "It's like I manifested them or something."

Stew finished his beer and stood. "Let's go fuck them up."

Terry held out his hand. "Right. They took Andy apart like he was a sandwich. You and Dan go out the front and swing around behind them. I'll go down the back stairs and distract them."

"I'll go with Terry," said Kat.

Stew's eyebrows raced up his forehead. "Distract them? You? You'll end up dead, if you're lucky."

"Hey. I said I'd go with him. We'll be okay."

Stew shook his head. "You're both nucking futz."

"Relax, big guy. Terry and I will dazzle them with witty repartee and stall them until the real muscle shows up."

Dan smacked Stew on the arm. "Let's go." He left his watch on his desk and trotted down the front steps. Stew followed, shaking his head and muttering. "Like pigs to slaughter."

Terry took a deep breath and smiled at Kat. "You don't have to do this."

"Like hell I don't. We're going to mess those two up." She opened the door to the back stairs. "Come on."

Jason turned off the ignition.

"We just going to sit here and wait for them to come out?" Rhonda angled her head to look up at the third floor. "'Cause I've got to pee."

The back door to McGinnis Investigations opened and Kate burst out with Terry right behind her.

Jason wrenched the door open. "This shouldn't take more than minute."

Rhonda fumbled with the glove box. "Guns?"

Jason leaned over and slammed it shut. "No. We passed the cop station about a block ago. And we're not going to need them. Not for these two."

Kat and Terry stopped half the distance from the door to the truck, standing side by side.

Rhonda crossed in front of the truck and stood beside Jason. She leaned her head close. "What are they looking at? What are they doing?"

"Who fucking cares?" Jason clenched his fists and started walking toward Kat and Terry. "It'll be the last thing they see for a very long time."

"They've got to tell us where the girl is."

"Just before I break their jaws. You take the chick, I'll take the punk."

Terry held up a hand. "Hang on there, champ." He pointed with his thumb over his shoulder. "Really good, high quality CCTV cameras up there. With audio. Got a great shot of you dropping off Andy a few days back. Be careful what you say and do because even if the two of us end up dead, the rest of the team will track you down and gut you like fish."

Jason snorted. "I'll take my chances." He took another step

forward and registered Terry glancing past him. He shifted to look over his shoulder and his leg buckled as Dan drove a boot into the back of his knee.

He followed through with a knee to the back of Jason's head. It glanced off his ear as the big Brit rolled out of his reach and stood facing Dan.

"Cheap shot."

Kat jumped on his back and looped an arm around his neck and put him in a choke hold.

Stew ran at Rhonda and swung a hard right cross at her. She ducked and jabbed her left, knocking Stew back, out of breath. "Fuck. You're strong."

She rolled her shoulders and jump-lunged at Stew, bringing her elbow down to the top of his head. He raised an arm to deflect the blow and grabbed her by the waist with one arm and rolled onto the ground with her, coming to a stop with her under him.

He dropped his butt on her pelvis, a 30kg weight advantage, and grabbed her wrists with his right hand. Cocked his left and snarled. "What the hell are you two looking for now?"

She shifted her weight, rolled slightly to her left, swung a leg over Stew's right foot, locked it and rolled on top of him. She drove an elbow into his ribs as she settled and grabbed his throat with both hands. "Fuck you. Where's the girl?"

Stew grabbed her by the wrists and tried to dislodge her grip. "Jesus," he gasped. He struggled for air. Tapped her on the arm.

"You're not tapping out, bitch," said Rhonda. "The girl."

Stew looked past her shoulder, his vision blurring.

She heard a footfall behind her and dropped a shoulder and rolled, releasing her grip, as Terry swung a plank at her head. It glanced off her shoulder and bounced off Stew's forehead.

"Fucking hell, Ter." Stew scrambled to his feet as he rubbed his neck. "Trying to kill me?"

Rhonda walked slowly backward, keeping an eye on Stew. "The girl."

Terry patted Stew on the arm. "Dan needs help."

Stew looked over at Jason with a choke hold on Dan and Kat on his back. "Ah, shit." He ran at them. "Get off him, Kat. Now. Brace yourself, Dan."

Kat's eyes widened as Stew barrelled toward them. She released and jumped to one side, sprawling on the pavement as Stew hit Dan and Jason at speed. The three tumbled across the pavement, Jason's head bouncing off the asphalt as he hit.

Dan rolled to his hands and knees, gasping for air. "Thanks."

Stew held out a hand and helped him up. "Yeah. No problem." He nodded at Kat. "You're fast. You and Terry get the hell out of here before you both get hurt." Stew and Dan were between Jason and Rhonda and their truck. "Go."

"You don't have to tell me twice," said Terry. He grabbed Kat's hand and ran.

She pulled her hand free. "Pussy. I'm staying. This is Andy's daughter they're talking about."

Rhonda stepped forward, cracking her knuckles and chuckling.

"Let's go, pretty."

Dan put his hand out and stopped Kat. "Take off. It's over."

She scowled, smacked Dan's hand away and stood there.

"I said go. I don't want anyone else hurt."

"But - "

"Kat, go back to the office with Terry."

She shook her head, spat on the ground near Rhonda's feet and left.

Jason moved to follow and Stew blocked his path.

"Hang on, champ."

Jason sized up Stew. "Another day, mate." He reached in his pocket and threw Kat's mobile on the ground. "Nice try with this, though." He drove his heel into the screen. "We're not that stupid."

Stew jabbed a fist in his chest as he tried to walk past him. "Today. What the fuck was this about?"

Rhonda stood beside Jason. "Where's the girl?"

Dan glanced at Kat's retreating figure. He shook his head. "What girl?"

Jason lunged at Dan and punched at his face. Dan twisted out of the way, Jason's fist glancing off his cheekbone. Dan help Jason's momentum, pushing his shoulder and spinning him into Stew.

Stew pushed him away. "What girl? Are you looking for a date, mate?"

Jason pointed in the general direction of Terry and Kat departing figures. "Those two kidnapped one of my employer's … maids."

"I think you've got the wrong people, pal. But hey, the coppers are just down the road. Wait here and I'll call them and we can sort this out now," growled Dan.

Jason wiped the corners of his mouth. He glanced at Rhonda who shook her head. "Another day. Trust me on this. You won't know when."

He pushed past Dan and Stew, Rhonda in his wake.

Dan shook his head at Stew. "Let them go."

"Don't come back," said Dan. "We won't be so nice the next time."

Jason paused getting into his truck, considering something, then discarding it. He slammed the door shut, accelerating out of the parking lot as Rhonda yelled something at him, pulling her door shut.

Chapter Twenty-Six

As soon as the truck left the parking lot Dan scooped the busted phone off the ground, ran to the back stairs and took them three at a time to the office. "Kat, are you okay?"

She was in the office kitchen holding a tea towel full of ice to the side of her head. He tossed her broken phone on the table. She dropped the ice and glared at Dan. "What do you think I am, some little kid? I could handle myself out there." She picked up her phone. "Shit."

"I'll get you a new one."

"I don't care about that. We can't track them now."

"How's your head?"

"It's fine. Bit of a lump. Bounced it off the pavement when I jumped off your back. Why'd you let them go?"

Stew exhaled and sat across from her. "It was going to be a stalemate. We'd pound the crap out of each other, but neither would win. And the cops were only a block away. There'll be another chance."

"Stalemate without Terry and I. We could have tipped the balance."

Stew blinked and rubbed his throat. "That would have been terrible for both of you. Nothing personal, but either one of them would have dispatched the both of you with one hand. Whatever advantage you would have provided would have been at the expense of your life." He shook his head. "Not having that."

He pushed himself to his feet. "Terry, dig deeper on the black web, or dark web, or whatever it's called. They must be having their sale soon if they're hurting that bad to find Kelly."

Dan nodded. "And Andy needs to know they're getting close." He unlocked his phone. "Don't worry about the feds finding out what you're doing, Ter. I'll let them know it's part of a case."

Jason pressed hard on the accelerator as he merged onto the highway north toward Sydney. The truck surged as he changed lanes in front of a heavy tractor-trailer. The airhorn startled him and he stuck his hand out the window and flipped the driver the finger.

"You'd lose that fight, mate," said Rhonda.

Jason stared at her.

"Watch the road."

He checked front, slowed, swerved to another lane to the right and accelerated again. He clenched his jaw and stared forward.

Rhonda sighed. "You want to turn around and kick their arses?"

He shook his head. "That's not what I'm thinking."

"I know. You going to call him or do you want me to?"

He exhaled, puffing out his cheeks. "Wasn't thinking about that, either."

"What then?"

Jason glanced her and passed another tractor trailer. "The girl there said it was Andy's daughter we were looking for."

"Who's Andy?"

"Look at that website again."

Rhonda navigated on her phone to the McGinnis Investigations website and clicked on the "Our Team" page. "Fucking hell. What are the odds?"

"Makes sense now why he was snooping around. Her daughter is in this."

A smile slowly filled her face. "I was afraid we were going back empty handed."

Jason nodded, settled back in his seat and set the cruise control. "We need a plan of attack, though. Something smarter than brute force."

"So what's the plan?" Rhona was sitting half-sideways, a foot up on the dash, the shoulder belt wrapped around a hand.

Jason looked at his watch. "Got an hour to work one out."

"It's getting dark. I'll call ahead."

Jason nodded. "We need the tech nerd, whatever his name is, there."

Prescott quivered with fury. "This is absolutely, unequivocally UNACCEPTABLE." He paced in his living room, a dark leather and mahogany, a 1980's version of what he thought rich was. "You failed twice now? Unacceptable."

He stopped in front of Jason. "What's your explanation?"

"I have none. But I have a plan."

He returned to his pacing "No explanation. A useless sack of barely sentient muscle." He threw a disgusted glance in Jason's direction. "You couldn't plan a root in a brothel. You have a plan?" Sarcasm dripped. He wheeled on him again. "That's your problem. Stop using whatever excuse for intelligence resides inside that abnormally thick skull and use your muscles. Like I hired you to."

Jason bunched his forearm muscles, clenching his fists. Rhonda tapped him on the arm and shook her head.

"He's got a pretty good plan," she said. "You should maybe listen."

"Oh, so the girl's talking for you now. Fine. What's this brilliant plan that redeems you?"

Jason took a couple of stabilising breaths. Shook out his hands. "You know that guy we caught snooping around the house in Kenthurst, and dumped back in Campbelltown?"

"What about him?"

"His name is Andy."

"Yeah, we know. So fucking what?"

"Let me tell this thing without interruptions, hey?" He rolled his shoulders. "That guy is the father of the girl what's missing. Number fifteen. That's probably why he was snooping around."

Prescott stopped pacing. "Go on."

"We know where he lives. He's got a couple of big, nasty friends who hang around to watch his back, or we'd have the girl now."

"What, you want more muscle?"

"No. We need to get his friends to leave him alone. He's still recovering from the beat down. Just him we can easily handle. Hell, even you could handle him." He held up his hand. "You know what I mean. They've got a smart tech guy on staff. We need to give him some bread crumbs. Enough to get the rest of them away for a few hours. Like I said. We know where he lives. We draw away the friends and we can grab the girl in about five minutes."

Prescott nodded. "Maybe you really aren't as dumb as you look. How do we do this?"

"We need an empty property owned by one of your shell companies."

Chapter Twenty-Seven

Andy paced with a distinct limp. "We're running out of time. That auction is going to be in the next couple of days. And we don't know where. The police are running around like chooks with their heads lopped off."

Dan was leaning back in his chair at the head of the conference room table watching him. "We can't stake out every place you know about."

"No, but we can rule some out by a process of elimination."

Terry and Kat were on the side of the table opposite Andy's pacing. They watched the anguish ripple cross his face.

Stew and Mac were on the same side as Andy. They gave up twisting in their chairs to watch him a couple of minutes ago.

"We should beat it out of them," said Stew. "I can find them."

"Them?" Kat was leaning forward. "The lovely couple ready to rip our heads off? The girls won't be near them. They've been placed in a holding area where they can be cleaned up, made ready for display. There'll be a couple of layers of security around the place. A smash and grab isn't going to work." She shook her head. "Jesus. I thought you'd know this."

Dan had a half smile on his face. "I think he meant to find Bonnie and Clyde, and beat the location of the girls out of them. I got that right, Stew?"

"So that's the plan?" Stew looked at Dan, frowning.

Andy sat at the table, rubbing his knee. "This isn't going to heal fast enough for me. Look, They pounded me when they found me at the place in Kenthurst, so it won't be there. That place has been blown."

"This is an auction for rich perverts, right?"

Dan and Stew nodded at Terry.

"So the Airds place is out of the question. Not the right kind of neighbourhood. A bunch of Beemers and Mercs would draw attention. Central Coast?"

All eyes turned to Mac.

He didn't notice for a second, then nodded. "There are some large houses up there, big land, lots of privacy, if you want to pay for it. It's finding the right place that's the challenge. Any ideas?"

Andy got up. "Hang on a second."

He went to the kitchen and summoned his wife and daughter.

Beryl came with them.

Kat and Terry stood and leaned against the wall, leaving the seats for the mother and daughter.

Beryl sat at the other end of the table, facing Dan. "We were enjoying a nice chat, Dan. What's this about?"

He shrugged. "Andy brought you in here. What's up, Andy?"

"Kelly, this might be difficult, but do you remember any of the places you were."

She looked at the faces staring at her. "Well, I was drugged most of the time. I was in a ship. I was in the house that I puked in. Then I was in a van for way too many hours, then a house on a farm, where Terry and Kat rescued me. Sorry, I can't really help." She blinked back tears. "I really want to help, though. Is there anything I can do?"

"Don't worry about it. It was just a thought. So we're looking at the Central Coast?"

Dan sighed. "Whoever is running this isn't living on the Central Coast. They may have property up there, but this kind of money finds beachfront on the Northern Beaches, or something at Potts Point."

"If we knew whoever is running this, we might have a better chance at finding what we need to find," said Terry.

Dan looked at Stew. They smiled at each other.

"So," said Dan. "Find out who owned the house in Airds, the place in Kenthurst, and see what else is in their name. You can do that, right?"

Terry closed his eyes and tilted his head back against the wall. "Shit. I should have thought of that. Give me an hour."

"You've got thirty minutes."

Terry bolted out of the room.

Andy slumped back in his chair. "So that'll identify all of the properties this sick fuck owns. Then what?"

"One step at a time, mate." Dan stood. "I need another coffee."

Christophe sat beside Jenny at a computer in Prescott's study. "More subtle."

Jenny shook her head. "Subtle? How in the hell do you make selling pre-teen girls subtle?"

"I don't know. I just don't want it really obvious."

"I'm on the dark web, Frenchie. This isn't crawled by Google. I know what I'm doing. Shut up and let me work."

"Will the invites actually go out?"

She stopped typing and glared at him. "I know what I'm doing. Shut up. Let me work."

Terry flicked between the many tabs he had open on his browser. He scribbled notes on a pad, then dropped his pen on the table and leaned back, smiling.

"You got something?" asked Kat.

"I've got something. These buildings, including the one we know about on the Central Coast, are owned by Samuel Prescott, personally or through a couple of different shell companies. Blue

Lagoon Properties and Bilitis Properties."

"Great," said Dan. "What else does he own?"

"And what on the dark web points to one of those properties?" Andy leaned forward. "Faster."

"I'm going as fast as I can." He grunted. "Property records are stored by council, not by state. This is going to take a bit."

"Check the councils where he's already got properties, and the adjacent ones."

"Thanks, Kat. Thought of that already. And thought of a faster way. They all use the same software. They all use a standard database structure and file path. Thank goodness for some semblance of uniformity. I've dragged all the databases locally and I'm searching them now. Couple of minutes."

Kat shrugged. "The easy part. Find an auction in the muck and I'll be impressed."

"I might miss some. The search parameters are pretty tight." Terry's laptop spit out seven results. The Airds property, Kenthurst, the gated house at Wamberal on the Central coast, plus four more. A home at Vaucluse, a flat in the city, a large house at Batemans Bay and another large house at Avoca, on the Central Coast.

"Even though Ryan raised the possibility, Batemans Bay is out of the question. Too far south. The girls were headed north. They were in Kenthurst. It's got to be Avoca," said Kat.

Terry's fingers flew over the keyboard. "Tor is launched. Looking for anything on the dark web related to any of Prescott's properties, but specifically those on the Central Coast, or at least north of

Sydney," He looked at Kat. "The trip north might have been a diversion. They could have doubled back."

Kat shook her head. "Stop second guessing yourself. They're not that clever. They're north of the city. No way they'd drive from Port Kembla all the way to Kenthurst, then double back to Batemans. No way."

"Batemans Bay is isolated."

Kat shook her head. "It's a three and a half hour drive from *here*. No way."

"She's right," said Dan. "Look for events north of the city."

Terry involuntarily shuddered. "This shit makes me feel dirty. I need a shower." He dug through user groups and web sites that should get him at least ten years in a federal prison if he was found out.

Dan was looking over his shoulder. "You're going to put us all in jail."

"I'm using Tor. Anonymised. The system thinks I'm in Lincoln, Nebraska. You're good."

"*We* better be good, or I've got a lot of explaining to do."

Terry lifted his head and stared directly at his boss. "Trust me. This is what you hired me for."

"Okay, okay. Finish up, quick, okay? You're making me nervous."

Terry grinned and continued his excavating. He visited a dozen different sites before he found what he was looking for.

"Okay, first, it's very disturbing how many sites there are out there set up solely to buy and sell people. Usually young girls, but a non-zero percentage were selling young boys."

"The girls. Get to it."

"Right, Andy. Relax." Terry regretted that word as soon as he saw the look on Andy's face. "Sorry. Right." He cleared his throat and sat back in his chair. He pointed at the monitor. "This address. Avoca Beach. Massive bloody house owned by Bilitis Properties. Someone is advertising a sale of unique and valuable objects at this address, tonight. Twenty-two lot numbers, with prices on fifteen of them. Seven up for auction. That has to be the place."

"Confidence level?"

"Can't put a number to it, but it's high. Really high."

Andy pushed back from the table. "Good enough for me. Let's go."

Dan grabbed him by the arm. "Oh, no, pal. Your body is still sticking its bones together. Take your wife and daughter home and re-connect. Heal. We can handle this."

"That's horseshit."

"Indeed it is. Suck it up. You're not coming with us."

Andy glared at Dan until Sophia tapped him on the arm. "Even if you were healthy, hun, which you're not, I still wouldn't let you go. Do get over it. You're taking Kelly and I to your place."

The lines on Andy's forehead deepened. "You know where I am. Call if you need anything."

Chapter Twenty-Eight

Dan stretched, extending his frame as much as he could in the small car. "Beautiful up here, but the drive is murder." He looked up at the two storey building. "This it?"

Stew nodded and turned off the ignition.

"Mac might not want to get involved," said Dan.

"He's an ex-cop. Human trafficking — sex trafficking — minors will definitely get him. He's old, but he's tough." He levered himself out of his car and stretched. "It is a bitch of a drive. I'll give you that."

They rounded the building from the parking lot and met Mac coming down the steel stairs from his office.

"Gents." He stuck out his hand. "Welcome back." He shook both of their hands, then pointed across the street. "Beer's over there. You're buying."

"We don't have time for food," said Stew, tight on his heels.

"There's always time." He led them into The Pelican. He nodded at Jessie, grabbed three menus off the wait stand and headed to the patio.

"You need to tell me what new information you have, and why you urgently need me. That'll take more than a minute. And I'm hungry. Eat when you can, right? Never know when the next opportunity will arise." He looked at his watch. "And it's almost lunch. They do a good schnitzel here."

They sat at a table near the railing, overlooking the marina.

"What's fast?" Stew settled in a chair and grabbed the menu. "The fish and chips any good?"

Dan took the menu from Stew's hands and dropped it on the table. "We're on a tight schedule, Mac." He unfolded a piece of paper. It was a screen grab from a satellite mapping program. "A big house in Avoca. We think the girls are there. Twenty-one of them. And where the girls are, the muscle is. You have anyone up here who can help?"

Mac pulled the paper over to his side of the table. Stew picked up the menu and glared at Mac, then raised his hand to signal the server.

"I'm pretty much a one-man show. There are some locals who help me out once in a while, but none of them are muscle. You have anyone else?"

Dan used his index finger to lower the menu blocking Stew's face.

"Terry?"

"And Kat. She's smart and tough."

Dan grimaced. "Neither would be considered muscle."

"Kat's motivated. She really want to take these fucks down."

Dan nodded and looked at his watch. "It'll delay us a couple of hours."

Mac jabbed his finger on the map printed out in front of him. "This place is about forty-five minutes back in the direction you came. Tell them to meet us there." He pointed on the map to a service station about half a kilometre from the house. "They can meet us there. We'll beat them by about 20 minutes."

Stew opened his phone. "I'll call them." He dragged the map across the table and worked out the address. "Terry. We're going to need you up here." He held up the map and oriented himself with the area. "Grab Kat and get up here as quick as you can."

"Kat's not available, big guy."

"She not well?"

"Jury duty. Started this morning. She's leaving for the courthouse in a couple of minutes. Out of commission for four weeks. I'll be there, though. Consider me gone."

"Okay. This is going to be hairy. Bring a weapon." He hung up and tossed the phone on the table. "Just Terry. No Kat."

"Ah, shit," said Dan. "Jury. Forgot. So it's the four of us."

"Look, guys, why don't we just call the cops?"

Kat had her backpack over one shoulder and was heading for the door when Terry took the call. She waited for him to finish the call.

"What was that?" she asked when he hung up.

"Stew. Wanted us to meet him," his phone warbled with a text message containing his destination, "in Avoca. At a servo close to the target. You've got jury, though, so it's just me." He frowned. "He said to bring a weapon. I don't have a carry license yet. Any ideas?"

Kat laughed. "Put your big boy pants on, Ter. You're in the big leagues." She adjusted her pack. "Hey, just in case I don't get selected, send me the address of the place. I might go up and join you. I'm in a mood for a fight."

"What's the case?"

She stopped. "Not sure." She pulled out the letter. "Any way you can tell from this?"

Terry checked the courthouse listings. "How many weeks?"

Kat leaned over his shoulder and pointed on the letter. "Four weeks."

"Right. Doesn't actually matter. There's only one trial starting today. *R v Leong Chang Yu*." He closed the laptop. "Hope that helps. I've got to run."

Kat had her phone out. "Hang on. Leong Chang what?"

"Yu. Y-U."

She typed a bit in her phone and frowned. "Okay." She read the results and scowled. "Send me that address, okay?"

"We can't call the cops. We don't have confirmation that this is the place. We have strong indications that it is, but that's not enough." Dan checked the time. "Terry is on his way. Let's go."

"We've got a twenty minute lead on him." Mac handed him a menu. "You won't regret it. Great food here. There's been rumours of this kind of shit up here for years. Never could get a grip on it. Always nebulous and impossible to nail down. If you've actually found the prick behind this foggy rumour, I'm with you 100%. But I'm starving. So order some food." He waved the server over. "Jessie will treat you right. Schnitzel for everyone."

Stew shook his head. "Fish and chips for me."

"BLT on Turkish for me," said Dan. "And a schooner of whatever's good."

Mac shrugged and handed the menus to Jessie. "Beers all around. Schnitzel for me."

Jessi tucked the menus under her arm. "Back in a jiffy, gents. And watch Mac. He'll try to rob you blind."

"Christophe, hurry it up, man." Jason straddled a chair, leaning on the back, right up in Christophe's face. "We're in a bit of a rush. We need to know where he lives."

The McGinnis Investigations 'About Us' page was open, scrolled to Andy's picture. Christophe shook his head. "A Private Investigation firm with their faces on their website. That is grade-A stupid. This guy doesn't look like a Smith. He's Indigenous. Definitely not a 'Smith'."

"I don't give a shit if he's a Petunia. Where's his home?"

"If *anybody* could do this, you wouldn't need my skills." His fingers flew over the keyboard.

Jason watched for a couple of seconds, then sighed and stood. "I thought everything was online. Easy to find with the click of a button. How much of what you're doing is for show?"

"You're pissed off because it's a problem you can't solve by punching it." Christophe looked up at the pacing Jason, raised an eyebrow and had a half smile on his face. "These guys are good. He's buried deep. You think I'm going to find a house in his name? Or the McGinnis company name?" He shook his head. "Of course not. There are layers, buried deep."

Jason checked the time again. "Look, I need to get going. Text me the address. It'll be down there somewhere."

Terry pulled into the servo in Avoca and parked beside Stew's blue Mazda. He hopped out of his car and into the backseat beside Dan. "Hey, guys. Thanks for waiting."

Stew started the car. "You had one more minute before we ditched you, kiddo."

Dan smiled. "Glad you could make it. You met Mac before?"

Terry reached between the front seats and shook his hand. "Yeah. Good to see you again. What's the plan?"

"We're going to check out the house,' said Dan. "Once we confirm they are there, and have the girls, we'll call the police. Four of us isn't a tenth of what we'd need to take a place this big. We scope the house out, confirm the contents. Mac knows the layout, he'll be our guide today."

Mac nodded in acknowledgement. "Head in from the north and park across the street. This place has a huge wrought iron gate at the front driveway, but it's for show. If the gate is closed, there's a quiet way in."

"Doesn't sound very secure."

Mac nodded as Stew pulled into traffic. "It's counter-intuitive. If you put on a big security show, people know there's something worth looking at. Keep the visible security at a minimum, and nobody is interested."

Stew parked half a block down the street from the target house. He rolled down the windows and cut the engine. He got out, raised the bonnet and pretended something was wrong with the engine.

Mac got out and stood beside him. "The gate is closed. Expected it. We won't be able to go through it."

Stew fiddled with a battery cable. "Captain Obvious reporting for duty." He looked at the house. It was a tall two storey with gables and chimneys at either end of the house. The curtains were drawn on all the windows. All of them still. "Place looks empty."

"We'll go around back. Close the hood."

"How?"

"It's quite simple, Stew. Move that lever out of the way and - "

"Arsehole, what's the way around back?"

Mac smiled. He spread the map on the hood of the car. "Terry and I will head down the drainage ditch to the south and get to the beach.

Dan, you and Stew cut through the church half a block to the north and get to the beach. We'll come around from the back."

Terry shook his head. "How are we going to get past any men they have in the back?"

"We're not." Stew nodded at Mac. "We go in low and slow. We see any guards, any security, tripwires, floodlights, anything like that and we slip back out and call the authorities."

"And if there's nothing there?"

"We go in and have a look." Dan put one of his headphones in. "We go in pairs. Mac keep your ears on. Stew grab a bag of goodies."

They split and quietly made their way, pincher style, along the beach and to the back of the house. The progress was slow, but steady. Stew and Dan met up with Mac and Terry and settled down behind some bushes on the back side of the property.

"Nothing," said Terry. "No floodlights, no nearly invisible tripwires, no guards. Nothing."

Dan looked pointedly at him. "Right. You've narrowed the locations down to this one, though. Right? Only possible option?"

"Only one that came up. We should go in. Check it out."

"Why would we do that now, Terry? We've been fucked with. Someone wanted us up here, out of the way. This place looks like it's been empty for weeks, if not months." Dan shook his head. "You take Mac back to his place and meet us back at the office and we regroup. Again."

"You're not getting rid of me that easy, Dan-o. I'll ride back with Terry. I'm seeing this through to the end."

Chapter Twenty-Nine

Kat spent the fifteen minutes it took to walk to the courthouse searching news on Leong Chang Yu. Google didn't paint a pretty picture. He'd been arrested a number of times for living on the earnings of prostitution, running an unlicenced brothel, assault, some petty theft. She recognised the face. He was in the kitchen at the chicken restaurant.

She placed her wallet and mobile phone in the small container at the security checkpoint in the courthouse. Her rings and necklace joined them. Then her small knapsack.

She waited for the security guard to wave her through. Green light, all clear. She collected her belongings and walked into the prospective jurors' waiting area. The room wasn't any larger than a middle-grade classroom. Eight rows of six chairs faced a low stage at the front of the room. A large monitor hung on the wall behind an empty podium. The state emblem filled the screen.

Kat looked at the clock on the wall. 12:42. She'd be called in twenty minutes or so. She was meant to be there by 1:00. And half of the prospective jury hadn't arrived yet. She picked a seat at the back of the room and opened her book.

A young man sat beside her, cocked his head to read her juror slip. "You're Katherine, right?" He held out his hand. "I'm Chris."

She smiled and shook his hand. "Hi Chris. Call me Kat, though.

"Okay. Kat." He read the spine of her book. "*Skystone*, eh? Never heard of it."

She flipped the book closed. "Historical fiction. Reimagining the whole King Arthur's court story."

"I'm more of a sci-fi, speculative fiction kinda guy."

"You might like it." She looked over her shoulder. "So what do you know about the case?"

Chris looked confused. "What's to know? The letter said four weeks. Nothing else in there. We aren't supposed to know, right?"

Kat shrugged. "It's not hard to find out. All trials are listed. There's only one starting today. The defendant is a piece of shit." She smiled. "I might be biased. Probably won't get picked."

Chris frowned. "You know the defendant?"

"Not *know* really. I've eaten at his chicken place. Just the once." She shivered. "Massive creep."

A couple more prospective jurors entered the waiting room.

"We should talk about something else." Chris looked over his shoulder. "So you're into that King Arthur stuff, are you? Camelot and all that?"

Kat closed the book and dropped it into her bag. "Yes. A time of chivalry and honour."

"And no showers and rotten teeth. Lifespan in the 30s, if you're lucky." Chris laughed. "It's an interesting story, though. It's a mythology that's lasted this long." He looked at the floor for a second. "So any idea what he's on trial for?"

Kat thought about the girl she found behind the restaurant. "I can guess." She crossed her arms and leaned back in her chair. "So what's your book? The one you go back to every couple of years?"

Chris thought a minute. "*The Stainless Steel Rat*. By Harry Harrison. Futuristic con man." He grinned. "Good light sci-fi and really funny."

"Not big into the science fiction." More prospective jurors arrived. "You think this'll go the full four weeks?"

"That's what the letter said."

Kat winced. "Not what I mean. These slime balls seem to get away with this shit all the time. You rarely hear about a conviction."

"You think it'll go longer?"

She shook her head. "Opposite. I think it'll be over faster than a bee's fart."

Chris put his hand on her arm and stopped her. "We can't talk about the case. Assume it's going to be four weeks."

Kat slumped back in her chair. 'Yeah. Probably."

Kat looked up from her book and glanced at the big clock on the wall. It was closing in on 2 p.m. She slowly closed her book around her index finger and looked around the room. "What the hell is going on? We should have been in there an hour ago."

Chris raised his arms over his head, stretched and yawned. "Yeah, something's happening. But maybe this is normal. Haven't been on a jury before."

"Fair point." She opened the book and looked for her spot. "Me either." She settled back into her chair and started reading where she left off.

She was another paragraph in when a uniform walked into the room from a side door and stepped onto the slightly elevated stage.

He knocked on the lectern with his knuckles. "Good afternoon, all. Thank you for performing your civic duty and showing up for jury service. You're probably wondering what's taking so long."

Kat nodded and spoke out of the side of her mouth at Chris. "We were right. It was taking too long."

The court officer continued talking. "Trials are unpredictable things. We expected this to go for three to four weeks. The defendant pleaded not guilty and witnesses were lined up. This morning it was made known to the court that one of the key prosecution witnesses will not be testifying. The charges have been dropped and the trial is now over."

Kat closed her book and absent-mindedly dropped it her bag. "Piece of shit."

He continued. "This information is confidential. You are not to share this information with anyone until you see it on the news or in print." He smiled. "Unfortunately, you won't be getting your daily jury allotment. Please make sure you notify your employers to ensure that amount isn't docked from your pay. Thank you again for your service. You won't be called again for at least twelve months."

He smiled at everyone again, stepped off the small raised area and left the room.

Kat threw her bag over her shoulder. "Well, it's been a slice, Chris. Have a nice life. This is bullshit."

"You're pissed because the trial was shortened? You wanted to be here four weeks?"

"I'm pissed that someone charged with human trafficking and child abuse got the charges dropped. The guy is a sketchy shit ball."

"Wait. How do you know that's what it was?"

"The defendant. The underaged girl he beat up and left in the garbage behind his restaurant. He looks like the kind of shit bag who would do that. Really pissed off I didn't get a chance to put him in jail."

She pushed her way past the other jurors and out of the room. "Son of a bitch." She dug her phone out of her bag and scrolled to Dan's number. She stepped around the corner toward the exit and quickly stepped back, phone in her hand forgotten. Just outside the courthouse, in a quiet corner, Leong, the man formerly in trial, the guy who owned the chicken shop, was shaking hands with the Federal cop, Tim Ryan.

"Shit."

She slowly raised her phone to chest level and opened the camera app. Took half a dozen pictures of Ryan and Leong Chang Yu.

"You absolute piece of shit."

Chapter Thirty

Andy pulled into the driveway of the small bungalow. It was at the end of a cul-de-sac in Glen Alpine, just south of Campbelltown. He shook his head, slightly, at the overgrown lawn and put the car in park. "Just so you know, I wasn't expecting company. And I've been really focussed on the business. Or in the hospital." He looked at Sophia, sitting in the passenger seat, then in the rear-view mirror at Kelly, sitting in the middle of the back seat. "Hey, are you wearing a seatbelt?"

"Just undid it." The girl pushed the car door open and stood in the drive looking at the house. "It's cute. Needs some paint."

Andy groaned as he opened the door and grunted himself out of the car.

"You okay?" asked Sophia.

"Aches. Pains. Old age."

"You were abused, dad. Lucky to be vertical, I think. What's the inside look like?"

"Messy. But it's home."

"Kinda tiny. I mean compared to what mum and I live in back home."

Andy grimaced as he limped up the walk to the front door. "They're a lot cheaper to buy back there." He unlocked the front door. "This does me just fine."

Sophia put her arm around her daughter's shoulder and pulled her close. "It's fine, Andy."

He smiled as he unlocked the front door. "It is." He took a deep breath. "Home Sweet Home, as humble as it may be." He held the door open as his wife and daughter entered.

The air inside was stale.

"Smells like man." Sophia pulled open the venetian blinds and cracked open windows.

"You'd prefer it smelled like women?"

Kelly chuckled as her mother slowly turned, one eyebrow arched.

Andy held up his hands. "Just kidding, sweets. Just kidding."

"Where are we going to sleep, dad?"

"I've got a cot in my office. You can take that. Or the sofa. Your mother and I sleep in my bed."

"Gross," said Kelly.

"I'll shower first."

Kelly shuddered and opened the fridge. Three bottles of beer, a half used tub of chip dip and some leftover pizza. She shook her head and swung the door closed. "There's nothing in here to eat."

Andy slowly walked over to his daughter and held her by the shoulders. "Am I ever glad to see you two. I was terrified I'd never see you again, young lady." He pulled her in for a hug, enveloping her small frame with his burly body.

Sophia joined them in the hug. "It's been too long since we've been together."

Andy sniffed, gave them both one last squeeze and pulled free. "Pizza? I can order. Vegetarian, right?"

"Don't change the subject, Andy."

"Actually, mum, I'm starved."

Andy opened an app on his phone and placed an order. "Getting some wings, too. And some soda for you, Kelly." He looked at his wife. "There's a nice red in the cupboard above the fridge."

Sophia took a deep breath. "Our daughter needs her father around. I think it's time we raised our daughter together."

Andy nodded. "I agree. I've been thinking that myself. So do I move to Cambodia, or are you two going to move here?"

"My business is running itself. I've got a good team working there. It makes more sense that we move. Kelly has been interested in coming here." Sophia crossed her arms. "How could you possibly continue what you do if you left Australia?"

Andy sat at the small dining table. Kelly and Sophia joined him. "Kelly is safe. The only thing that is important is that Kelly is safe.

I had some time to think while I was hooked up to the hospital bed. I swore I'd pack it in if I found you." He took Kelly's hands. "And I found you. So, I'm going to retire, sell out my share of the business to Dan and find something far less exciting to do."

Sophia shook her head. "No."

"Don't worry about money. I've got transferrable skills."

"I don't need your money, you idiot. I've got plenty of my own. And you're not going to sell out. You can't."

He sat back in his chair. "I need to get out of this racket. I can't have my family hurt like this. We're lucky Kelly is safe."

"No thanks to you." Sophia held up a finger to shut his mouth. "A couple of your colleagues, much younger that you, got her out. And there are –" she looked at Kelly, "-- how many?"

"Twenty-one more."

"Twenty-one other girls who need to be rescued from that horrible situation before god only know what happens to them."

"I know what will happen to them, mum. I'm not a kid."

"You *are* a kid and you should never need to know about these things."

Andy slumped in his chair and sighed. "Dan and the team are more than well equipped for this. I hurt. I'm tired. And I don't want to put either of you in any more danger."

Sophia reached across the table and smacked him on the shoulder. "If you want to quit, quit after you get the girls back."

He winced and rubbed his shoulder.

"I'm not sorry," said Sophia.

"I gathered." He looked at his wife, holding her gaze. She had that determined look he'd known for over a dozen years now.

He sniffed and nodded. "Okay. You two need to get somewhere safe, a long way away from here. The mutts who took you, who did this to me, aren't going to be too pleased with your rescue. They'll want you back, Kelly, and will do anything to anyone to make that happen."

Sophia slowly exhaled. "I don't like this. But you're right. We'll stay here tonight and find a hotel tomorrow."

"There are some nice ones in the city. You two can play tourist while I rescue a bunch of damsels in distress."

The doorbell rang at the same time as an alert chimed on his phone.

"Pizza is here."

Andy passed the almost empty pizza box to his daughter and sat back in the chair at the small dining room table. "Finish it. I've had too much."

She snatched the last wedge from the box and dropped it on her plate. "Thanks."

He leaned forward, elbows on the table and his fingers intertwined with Sophia's. "There are some nice hotels in downtown Sydney. Nice and busy. Plenty of crowds. I'll call a nice one and make a reservation for a couple of nights."

"We're fine here. We're safe here," said Sophia.

Andy shook his head. "These are very dangerous people. I don't know what they know. And they are very upset. At me." He lifted his shirt and displayed the broad bandage holding his ribs together and the deep purple bruises either side of it. "And they will try to get to me through the two of you."

Sophia glanced at Kelly. "Not in front of her."

"Mum, I'm not a kid. I know what they are doing. They took me, remember?" She took another bite. "I am fine heading into the big city, you and I can go shopping, and Dad and his friends can find those arseholes and beat the shit out of them. For me." She swallowed pizza and smiled. "You can do that, right? Get the rest of the girls then beat those guys up?"

"Kaliyanei, don't talk like that."

"What? Mum? You want to give them hugs and kisses on their cheeks? They need to be punished."

"That's what the police are for."

Andy winked at his daughter, with the eye his wife couldn't see. "She's right, Kelly. That's for the police. We'll get the girls back and set them up for the police. No beatings, no fights. I'm getting too old for that crap anyway. About time to cash out and retire."

Sophia ran her fingertips down his arm. "Not that old."

"Gross." Kelly wiped her fingers on a paper towel. "I'm sleeping on the sofa, aren't I?"

Sophia chuckled. "Or we get the cot out. It's a little early yet. Where's the wine, Andy?"

Kelly sat on the sofa, legs curled under her scrolling through something on Andy's phone.

Andy took his wife's empty wine glass and placed it and his in the kitchen sink. "We need to call it a night. Early day tomorrow. I want to show you around the waterfront before we put you in that hotel."

"I still think you're over-reacting to this. It can't be that bad."

The front door smashed open and Rhonda followed Jason in. Kelly screamed and jumped behind the sofa. Sophia jumped out of her seat and put the table between them.

Andy slowly stood. "You two again. What the fuck?" He picked the wine bottle up by the neck. "I owe you both a beating. Soph, call the police. It's triple-zero."

Rhonda lunged for Sophia and Andy lashed out with the wine bottle. Rhonda raised her right arm to block and it bounced off her wrist. She let out a whelp as Sophia back-pedalled, tripping and falling hard on her backside.

Rhonda cradled her wrist. "Jesus Christ, that hurt. Right on the bone."

Andy raised the wine bottle to follow through and Jason crash-tackled him, driving him into the table and falling with him to the floor.

Andy was face down, wine bottle under chest and Jason on his back. The wind was knocked out of him. He tried to take a breath and winced. "Ribs. Shit." He tried to roll and Jason forced his neck down with his forearm.

"Stay." He nodded at Rhonda. "Grab the woman. And where's the fucking girl?"

Andy grunted through the pain and heaved upward, trying to dislodge Jason. He got the wine bottle free and slid it across the floor to Sophia. "Make her bleed."

Sophia grabbed the bottle and rolled to her feet swinging. Rhonda ducked and punched, knocking the wind out of Sophia and driving her into the small kitchen.

Andy grimaced, rolled to stand and saw stars as Jason kicked him in the head.

Dan watched the paramedics load Andy into the ambulance for the second time in a week. He waited until it sped off, lights flashing, siren wailing, before turning back to Peters. "What do you have?"

The cop shrugged. "There was a fight. Big one, by the looks of it. CSU will be pulling prints and gathering trace, but best info will come from Andy when he's out of surgery. Neighbours heard yelling and smashing and called it in."

"Where are his wife and daughter?"

Peters shook his head. "No sign. We're hard on it."

"Human trafficking, sex slaves, shit that sticks all the way up the coast. I hate this."

His phone rang. Kat. He sent it to voicemail.

"How far have you gotten? Who's behind this?" asked Peters.

"I thought that was your job, mate." His phone rang again. Kat, again. He held up a finger and answered. "Kat, I'm busy. Aren't you on jury duty?"

"Charges dropped. Key prosecution witness no longer available to testify.”

“Okay, so head back to the office and catch up with Beryl.”

“Where are you if you’re not in the office?”

“Andy’s place. He’s on the way to the hospital and his wife and daughter are missing.”

“The fuck? Is he okay? Do the police know where Kelly and Sophia are?”

“He’s pretty bashed up. And no. No clue where they are. A CSU team is scouring the place. Head back to the office. We’re back at square one.”

“Not quite square one. The shit is getting deeper. I’ll see you there.”

“What do you mean, not quite square one? Deeper? Hello? Kat?” He looked at his phone. She’d hung up. “What the fuck?”

Chapter Thirty-One

The ambulance arrived at Campbelltown Hospital and Andy was hustled into the Emergency department.

Beryl waited while he was wheeled in and followed. "Jesus, mate. Dan said you were bad, but this is nuts."

Andy's eyes were swollen, almost shut. Blood caked his hair and was drying on his shirt. He took a shallow, shuddering breath. "Find them. You've got to find them."

The paramedic gently moved her to one side and led the gurney into the examination room. "You'll need to wait out here. He's going to be prepped for surgery. Leave your number at the nurses' station and they'll contact you with his status."

Beryl nodded and unlocked her phone while she walked to the

nurses' station. "Dan, he's in bad shape."

"Let me talk to him."

Beryl shook her head and leaned on the nurses' station counter. "He's going straight into surgery. Orbital shattered. I'm not going to hear from him for hours. I'm heading back to the office after I give them my contact details. See you there?"

"Yeah. The CSU team is going to be here for a while."

"Before he went in he mumbled something about finding them. How's that going?"

There was a long pause on the line. Then a sigh. "Not well. I'll meet you back at the office. We need to start over with this."

Dan slapped both hands down on the conference table. "Son of a bitch. How does this guy stay ahead of us? We're not that stupid."

Terry, Beryl, Stew, Mac and Kat sat around the table.

"I'll tell you how," said Kat. "That trial I was supposed to be on. Human trafficking. The chicken shop guy was the defendant. Supposedly, according to whispers, a slam dunk case. That girl I found was one of the victims. I think she was the key witness and now she's in a coma. When the case was dropped I saw him and the Fed having a good old chummy chat."

Dan sat back in his seat, stunned. "Not Wazza?"

Kat shook her head. "Just the Fed. Ryan, whatever. I never liked that prick."

Dan pushed his chair back and ran his fingers through his hair. "Shit, shit, shit."

"We've got to call Wazza," said Terry.

Dan held up his hand. "Not yet. We need to think this through. Jesus. Who else?" He wiped his face and slapped the wall. "We're running out of time. This is happening tonight or tomorrow. Or not at all. If we don't find those girls today, they're gone." He held a finger. "And that's not going to happen."

Andy looked through swollen eyelids at the surgeon. "Will I be able to play piano again, doc?" He was on the operating table idly watching the bustle as he was prepared for surgery.

The surgeon smiled. "As well as you did before. I'm Doctor Swain. How's your vision?"

Andy grunted. "I've got slits for eyeholes. How do you think my vision is?"

"X-rays show broken bones on your face. Specifically the left orbital socket. You got bashed pretty hard. You're getting too old for this shit."

"Hey. That's my line." He took a shallow breath. "Doing anything about my ribs while I'm under?"

The surgeon shook his head. "Just fractures. They'll heal well enough on their own."

"When will I be able to get out of here?"

"Do you have private insurance?" The doctor smiled. "As long as I don't mess up, you'll be out of here in a few days. A week at the most."

"Oh, hell no." Andy looked at the cannula on the back of his hand

and tried reaching over to pull it out. His arms were too weak.

"Don't do that, mate." The surgeon gently pushed Andy's arm back on the operating table. "What's the rush?"

"The guy -- and woman -- who did this to me took my wife and daughter. I can't lie around doing nothing about it."

"Your first priority is to let me fix you up. I'm sure your friends are doing everything they can."

"They have no idea what those two are capable of."

"This is the second time you've been in here in the past week. I'm sure they know." He pointed to the anaesthesiologist. "That's Dave. He's going to keep you alive while I patch you up. His job is much easier if you're calm and relaxed. So be calm, and relax." He checked a note on the chart. "I'll call Beryl myself as soon as we're out of here, okay?"

The anaesthesiologist attached a feed to the cannula and taped it in place. "I'm going to give you a sedative, Mr Smith. Just to make sure you're relaxed."

"I'm already relaxed."

"Great. Still going to do it. I'll be at your head the entire time making sure you come out the other end of this. I've been doing this for years. When's the last time you ate?"

"Pizza and a couple of beers about two hours ago."

"How many slices?"

"Three."

"Beer?"

"Two. And two glasses of red."

"Thanks. Good thing we talked first." He nodded at Swain. "We're ready to go."

Andy opened his eyes to Beryl standing over him. "Jesus, woman. You scared the shit out of me."

"How are you feeling?"

"Like I was passed through a wood chipper and reconstituted by Picasso. How do I look?"

Beryl considered his face. "Same same."

"You're a sweetheart. Give me a sitrep."

She handed him a glass of chipped ice and sat beside the bed. "Most of the team are trying to find the location of the imminent auction. Mac is helping. They're going hard. Don't worry. They'll find Kelly and Sophia."

"What did the surgeon do to me?"

Beryl got up from the chair and checked the chart. She shrugged dismissively. "Mostly orbital socket surgery. You'll have black eyes for a week or so, but the rest of you is pretty much good to go. Except for the ribs. Cracked and bruised, but not a danger."

"I feel like shit."

She winced. "Probably those ribs."

He pushed himself up to the sitting position, wincing. "Nothing else?"

She shrugged. "Nothing major."

He pulled the cannula from his hand and the sensors from his chest and swung his feet off the bed. Braced himself as he stood.

"We're out of here. I can't stay in here while my girls are missing."

"I'm not going to stand in your way, but I think you're a bloody idiot."

"Of course you do. And I probably am." Andy shucked off his hospital robe and winked at Beryl. "Don't get too excited. Your heart, you know." He pulled on his trousers and a blood stained T-shirt. "You've got a ride here, right?"

"This is a bad idea."

"All my ideas today are going to fall into that category." Andy grabbed the chart and unclipped the pen from the top. Wrote a note across the top sheet. *I've checked myself out. Thanks for all the great work you did.*

He signed it and dropped the clipboard on the bed. "Let's get the hell out of here."

Kelly and Sophia were in a small, spare room with a couple of chairs, a small table and a mirror covering half of one wall. Small speakers were mounted in two ceiling corners.

"That's a two-way mirror, mum." Kelly paced in front of it with her arms crossed. "They're probably watching us and listening to everything we say." She spat on the glass and turned back to her mother. "Are you okay?"

Sophia had a small lump and bruise on her forehead. Her blouse was ripped and spattered with blood. She furrowed her brow. "I'm fine. These are the same people who grabbed you before?"

Kelly nodded. "Yeah. Well, technically I was grabbed back home, but the big ugly guy is part of that group of bastards."

"We need to get a message to the police."

Kelly shook her head and pulled the other chair close to her mother. "I think the police are in on this," she whispered. "And I'm pretty sure they can hear us. Don't worry, though, I've got—"

"STOP WHISPERING," yelled a man's voice through the speakers. He cleared his throat. "Young lady, you've been a major pain in my arse."

"Show your face, coward."

"Feisty. Mum, tell your daughter to mind her manners or it won't be pretty."

The door opened. Sam Prescott and Jason walked in. Kelly lunged at Prescott and was stopped by Jason.

"Don't bruise her," yelled Prescott. "Be careful. She's valuable."

"Don't bruise her because I will eviscerate you if you touch my daughter again." Sophia pushed Jason back. Or tried to. He barely budged.

He grabbed her by the wrist and threw her to the floor. "I can kill this one now."

Prescott shook his head. He reached out a hand to help her up. She refused his help, spat at his shoes and pushed herself to her feet. "She's feisty. I think I'll add her to the menu. A last minute surprise. Maybe I could throw her in as a sweetener. A mother - daughter package might get me a lot more than I could get for each of them individually."

"Drop dead."

Prescott nodded at Jason. "Put them both with the others."

He turned to leave and Jason grabbed him by the arm. "You sure?" he asked, his voice low.

"Yes. I'm sure."

"They're a handful."

Prescott closed his eyes in exasperation. "Lace their water, idiot. And soon. Move it."

Chapter Thirty-Two

Dan was at his normal place at the head of the table. Beryl, Stew, Kat and Terry, all of them amped up, sat around the table in the conference room.

Andy stood at the opposite wall. Beryl looked at him and pulled out a chair.

He shook his head. "Thanks. I'll stand. If I stop moving it might be permanent." He coughed and winced, holding his ribs. "What's the sitrep?"

"We've got two problems," said Stew. "Two overarching problems, each containing dozens of little problems."

"Listen to Mr Cheery here." Andy stretched out his ribs. "What's the bad news?"

Stew ignored him. "Problem one, find and get the girls. Problem two, find and take down every single son of a bitch involved with this."

Kat raised her eyebrows. "Take down means kill, right?"

"Get them in jail. The inmates will take care of them."

Kat looked like she wanted to volunteer getting arrested. She grunted. "Whatever."

"And we're quickly running out of time." Dan pointed at Terry. "You stay here. Go through everything. Every single thing linked to this Prescott guy. Find out what he knows, what he's set up in partnerships, everything. We need to find a place that can comfortably hold more than 20 girls, and is high scale enough to host an auction."

"What are you doing?"

"Stew and I are heading back up to the Central Coast. Probabilities skew to this all happening up there. Text us whatever you find."

"I'm going with you," said Kat.

Dan shook his head. "No can do."

"Because I'm a girl?"

"Because this is not your strength. You build us websites, fake identification. This is a little more serious."

"I'm the only one here who has met the other girls. I told them I'd be back to help them. They'll trust me. You don't have a choice. I need to go with you."

Dan stared at her for a few seconds.

"She's right, Dan."

He glared at Stew. "Yeah. I hate it." He nodded. "We leave in ten minutes."

"I find the right place, I'm going to be right behind you," said Terry.

"The more the merrier." Dan nodded at Andy "You haven't said anything yet. You look like a racoon."

"I'm not staying here. Sorry if you thought any different. My wife, my kid. I'm not staying here."

"You couldn't knock a toddler off a trike. You're going to be more trouble than you're worth."

Andy shrugged. "I go with you or I go on my own. Doesn't matter which. I'll beat the address out of Terry if I have to."

"I think I might actually be able to take you, the state you're in."

"Don't bet against me, kid." Andy pushed off the wall. "What're we doing?"

"Hitting the Avoca place first and bugging it. They might plan on doubling back. Can't hurt to plant a couple or ten devices in there."

Beryl stood. "I'll put some packages together."

"All of the inventory. We're going to wire every place we can find for sound."

Stew pushed back from the table. "I'll call Mac. We're probably going to be hanging out up there for a bit."

Terry sat back from the computer and rubbed his eyes. He looked up at the almost empty office. Beryl was sitting at her desk with a cup of tea and an inquisitive look on her face.

"Any luck?"

He nodded. Shuffled the papers until he found what he was looking for. "The girls are probably at a farm he has west of Gosford. It's a large property owned by a shell company I hadn't linked to him before, but all of its funds come from Bilitis Holdings. It's a big house, Isolated from everyone. They weren't at the Avoca address, so this is the next best option." He typed a message in his phone. "I've got to let Dan know."

He piled the papers on his desk, slid them into a drawer and grabbed his keys. "I'm meeting them up there."

"Be careful."

"No, they're the ones who have to be careful."

"Don't get yourself killed, kiddo."

Dan, Kat and Andy were walking along the dunes behind the house. It was daylight now. Harder to sneak up on an occupied house. So they tried to act casual.

"It doesn't look occupied."

Dan looked at his friend, bruised and barely disguising a limp. "Fortunately for us. Mainly you." Stew and Mac were approaching them from the other direction. "And those two old guys."

"I heard that, Dan." Stew adjusted the pack hanging off his shoulder. "So it's broad daylight. How do we get in without drawing attention."

Mac shook his head. "Just walk the hell in, man. You guys

coming?"

Stew lurched forward and grabbed him by the shoulder. "Hang on, Einstein. We don't know the place is empty. We just know the girls aren't here."

Mac sighed. "No guards back here. No evidence of tripwires. It was empty less than 24 hours ago. They wouldn't have time to set up shop here that fast." He pulled himself free. "Let's get this done."

He wound his way through the scrub to the back of the house. Dan shook his head and followed.

Kat smiled. "I like this guy."

Andy picked the lock on the back door. They gathered in the spacious kitchen.

"Stew, Kat and I will hit upstairs, the rest of you cover down here, right? Doesn't look like Andy can make the stairs," said Dan.

"When I'm healthy again you're going to pay for that, mate." He grabbed half a dozen devices out of the bag hanging off Dan's shoulder. "While you're upstairs find a place to hide the transmitter."

"Aye, aye Cap."

Dan's phone warbled as he went up the stairs. He read Terry's message and held up his hand. "Hang on, hang on. Terry found an address, looks like about an hour west of here. Big farm house. Probably where the girls are held. Perfect location."

"Screw this place. Let's go," said Andy.

"We'll put a couple bugs in this place anyway. We're here. Stew, plant the transmitter and a couple of audio only receivers upstairs.

We'll plant some down here. Andy, find the office. I'll hide one here in the kitchen."

Andy hesitated.

"Come on, Andy. You know this is the smart thing. We'll be on the way in ten minutes."

"We're going out the front door. Car's closer. Won't have to walk so bloody far." Andy slid a chair from the dining room to in front of the cabinets above the fridge. He powered up the listening device, waited until it signalled its connection with the transmitter and placed it on top of the cabinet. He eased himself down from the chair and stood back. It was invisible to anyone shorter than 2 metres tall.

"Okay. We're going." He was halfway up the hall toward the front door when a shadow darkened one of the frosted side panel windows.

"Shit." He back-pedalled to the kitchen. "Dan," he whispered. Grabbed him by the arm and pulled him into the kitchen. "Someone is coming up the front steps."

"Dammit. Upstairs, as quickly and quietly as you can."

Andy hobbled up the stairs, gripping the bannister. Stew met them at the top landing.

"You guys finished down there? We're ready to go." Stew slung the bag over his shoulder and waited for Dan to head back down the stairs.

"Shut up," said Dan. "We're about to have company." He hustled them all to a bedroom at the front of the house. "We don't have the luxury of waiting them out." He looked at Andy. "And this guy is in no shape to jump."

Stew looked out the window. "This steps onto the porch roof. Easy descent from there with the downspout." He handed his bag to Mac. "I'll drop down and create a diversion, the rest of you head out the back."

"I'll do it," said Kat. "I'm lighter. Big guy here will rip the downspout off."

The front door opened and they heard two voices.

"Stew, give her your keys," whispered Dan. "Kat, be in the parking lot south of here in about five minutes."

Kat slid the sash window up and lowered herself onto the porch roof. Stew's car was about a block down the road. A black Toyota was parked in the driveway. She scrambled to the edge of the roof and tested the downspout. It was old, galvanised steel. A bit of a tug and a bracket loosened from the wood siding. "Okay, so not that way." She walked carefully around the edge of the tiles, treading that delicate balance between stealth and not falling off. The northernmost end hung over a large hedge.

She sighed. "Better than asphalt, I guess." She took a deep breath and jumped.

Shrubbery isn't the best cushioning material, but Kat escaped with nothing more than scrapes and scratches. She pulled twigs from the neck of her T-shirt and stumbled onto the driveway.

The Toyota was fairly new. She slid a knife from her back pocket and stabbed the sidewalls of the two back tyres, flattening them.

She dug around in the front garden until she found a large enough rock and threw it through the front window. She waited until the front door opened and two men came onto the front step before she started running.

She was in Stew's car and passing in front of the house, heading toward the parking lot, before the two at the house had discovered the flat tyres. She could hear them yelling foul things at her.

She smiled as she pulled into the beach parking lot. Nosed the car into a space up against the dunes and got out.

A short, wooden walkway bridged the path from the parking lot to the water, over the dunes. Kat stood at one end and watched as Dan, Stew, Mac and a hobbling Andy hustled their way across from the other side.

"You okay, Kat?" Stew held his hand out for the keys. "That crash into the bushes was pretty noisy."

"I'm fine. The bugs working?"

Stew held up the receiver. *Who the hell was that? This place is blown.* He turned it off. "I don't think the place is blown. They don't have many options left."

Dan entered the address Terry sent him into the car's navigation system. "It's just under an hour away. Terry will meet us there. We need to pull up short and scope the place out or we'll spook them."

Chapter Thirty-Three

Sophia and Kelly were shoved through a door, hoods on their heads and their hands tied in front of them. The door latched behind them.

Sophia pulled off her hood and pulled Kelly toward her. She took Kelly's hood off and untied the rope around her wrists. She held out her own wrists. "Can't do this my own. Are you okay?"

Kelly blinked in the light and looked around. They were in a small unfurnished room with no windows and two doors. She nodded. "I'll live."

"Do you recognise this place?"

Kelly fumbled with the rope. "Not a place I've been before. We need to get out of here before they drug us."

Sophia rubbed her wrists and checked the doors. The one they'd just come through was locked. The door on the opposite wall wasn't.

She pushed it open. It was like a minimum security prison. A large rumpus room-like area with twelve bunkbeds. Open showers were against one wall and a long, low table was on the opposite. A large fridge stood in a corner. Scraps of food littered the table. The girls were either sleeping in a bunk bed or sitting, vacant-eyed in a chair or against the walls. "This is purpose built."

Kelly rushed to one of the girls and slapped her gently on the cheek. Repeatedly. "Hey. Look at me. Do you remember me? Come on. Focus your eyes."

The girl looked away. Her eyes rolled back and she slumped to one side.

"Waste of time, Kaliyanei. Help me check this place for any surveillance. Before you talk to anyone else."

"Yes, *mteay*." She rolled her eyes and started checking the large room.

"Remember what *aupouk* said," whispered Sophia. "Look for air vents, hidden corners, telephones…"

"Mama, I know. I know. And I seriously doubt there will be any telephones here."

Sophia smiled. She grabbed a chair and checked light fixtures and air vents in the ceiling, the corners of the doorframe, and behind the moulding.

She watched as Kelly attempted to move the fridge. Hopped off the chair and helped her. She checked the space in the back where the compressor was housed. Checked on top. "Nothing so far."

Kelly pointed at the electric outlet plate. "Maybe?"

Sophia nodded and took inventory of the room's contents. No metal flatware. The food containers were cardboard. On one end of the table were some Chinese takeout containers. With thin, wire handles. "I think I've got something."

She removed the handle. The end was bent at a 90 degree angle. She jammed the corner into the slotted bolt head and loosened it. Took the faceplate off and checked. Clean. She handed a second handle to Kelly. "Start the other side and meet me in the middle. Keep it neat. Careful you don't get shocked. Put the faceplates back on when you're finished."

She put the plate back on and screwed in the bolt. Slid the fridge back into place, and scuffed up the streaks it left on the floor.

She moved counter clockwise around the room, Kelly moved clockwise.

They met at the far corner of the room.

"Nothing," said Kelly. "Strange."

"Nothing my side either." Sophia looked at the other girls. "Not that strange, maybe. These girls are so drugged there is nothing to listen to." She held up the wire handle. "We can get out with these. But we can't take the girls. They're too far gone."

Kelly shook her head. "I know. I hate it, but I know." She took a long look at the girls she had spent days with on the boat. "Okay. Let's go."

"Oh, no. Not yet. We need to wait until the food is brought to us. We need to hide our escape."

Kelly tipped her head back and groaned. "You've got to be kidding me."

"Sorry, daughter. We need to hide these wires too, and make sure they don't notice they're missing." She took the wire handle from Kelly and pulled out the fridge. She bent them to fit in the recess where the compressor sat, then slid the fridge back into place.

"Okay, the containers they were on. Where are they? We need to bin them."

Kelly grabbed them and a number of others and swept them into a large plastic garbage bin. Made like she was trying to clean the place up.

"That's great, honey. Now we need to wait until - "

The door opened and Vasily wheeled a trolley in. Ilya followed him. On the trolley were about 30 bottles of water. Sophia squinted and looked closely at the caps. They'd been loosened already.

Kelly leaned close to her mother and whispered. "Those are the two animals who bussed us up from the ship. They are Russian. The little one is Vasily and the other one is Ilya. They are pigs." She had a small smile. "I hit the big one with a car. Should have aimed better."

Vasily noticed Kelly. The smile on his face would curdle milk. "So you're back, number fifteen. I won't make the same mistake twice. Ilya, get the rest of them a bottle to drink. I'll deal with the little bitch and her bitch mother."

Sophia stood, defiant. Kelly stood up beside her and Sophia pushed her behind. "I normally like Russians, but for you two I will make huge exceptions." She bunched her fists. "You stay away from both of us."

"I think not, mama bitch. My boss likes his girls docile. And to be girl, not an old woman like you." He laughed at his joke. "You will each drink two bottle of this water. Double dose. No tricks like last time, little bitch. I'm going to watch you both drink two bottles."

"How are you going to make me? Your *boss* does not want us hurt."

"Easy." He squeezed his hand around Sophia's throat. "He doesn't want the girls hurt. He doesn't care about your mother." His hand tightened. Sophia grabbed at his wrist and struggled for air. "If the little bitch doesn't drink now, she will watch her mama bitch die in front of her eyes."

He picked two bottles off the trolley and threw them at Kelly. "Drink them both now. If you spill a drip, you will drink a third. Even just one drip." He eased off on Sophia's throat. "Mama bitch, tell her what happens if she doesn't drink all of the water."

She nodded at her daughter. "Do it. It'll be okay."

When Kelly finished the second bottle Vasily handed two to Sophia. "Now you. Or you die. Same rules. One little drip and it will be three bottles." He released her throat.

Ilya had finished administering to the others. He stood behind Vasily with his arms crossed and a smile on his face. "You better not be fucking this up this time, *tovarich*, or you will end up the dead one."

"You finished? Take the trolley out of here. I don't want them to think they might be able to make a weapon out of it."

Ilya laughed as he wheeled it out of the room. Sophia watched him leave as she drank.

Vasily watched her eyes, and shook a finger in her face. "No, no, no. You have no advantage with my big friend gone. I could snap your neck like a chicken bone. Finish the water and have a nice sleep. This will end for you tomorrow."

Sophia tipped the bottle back, catching the last drop, then threw the bottle at Vasily's face.

He ducked and laughed. "Maybe I can see why the boss wanted to keep you. I'm going now. Showers tomorrow morning at 6:00."

"What about food?"

"You won't starve in the next twenty-four hours, and after that you'll be somebody else's problem.'

He followed Ilya out and locked the outer door behind him, leaving the inner door between the dorm and the entry way open.

Sophia waited a minute until she was sure they had left, then grabbed Kelly and ran to the showers. At the end of the row of showers was a toilet and a sink. She turned on the faucet and pushed Kelly toward it. "Drink as much water as you can. Until you don't think you can drink any more, then vomit. Repeat it two or three times."

Kelly was blinking slowly. "It's already starting to hit me."

"Then go fast."

"There's only one sink. What about you?"

Sophia pushed her toward the sink. "Stop talking and do what I told you to do." She waited until Kelly complied then stood under a shower. Turned the cold water on full and opened her mouth. She swallowed as quickly as she could, sputtering and choking, then leaned over, stuck two fingers down her throat and retched. Repeated it until she'd heaved all of the water from her stomach. She wiped off her face and repeated the exercise.

She heard Kelly retching beside her. "Fill your stomach again, And then do it again."

She was bloated with water and retched again, vomiting another bellyful of water. She wiped off her face and let the shower wash away the mess while she turned to help her daughter. "You okay?"

Kelly leaned over and stuck two fingers down her throat. Her mother held back her hair. She retched a couple of times, then heaved up a stomach full of water all over the floor. "This is gross."

"How are you feeling? Alert enough?"

"Still a bit groggy. Let's get out of here." She wiped tears from her eyes. "I really don't want to do this again."

Sophia moved the fridge out of the way and retrieved the two take-away box handles. "Help me." Together they pushed the fridge back. She kneeled in front of the door and pressed her ear against it. Held a finger to her lips. "Sshhh."

"What happens if you open the door and there's an angry Russian on the other side?"

"I said shush." She closed her eyes and concentrated on everything she could hear. There were voices, but they were distant. "It sounds like nobody is close. When I open the door, stay very low until we can figure out our next step. They'll notice if we stand, but might not if we crouch."

She eased the thin metal wire into the keyhole, applying torsion with one while she worked the tumblers with the other. It took some time.

"You know what you're doing?"

"Your father taught me, but these are not the right tools. It's taking too long, but I'm almost there. Get ready."

Terry pulled up on the shoulder about half a kilometre from the large farmhouse. He called Dan. "I'm here. How far away are you?"

"Ten minutes out. What do you see?"

"This is the place. Hurry."

He hung up and peered at the property through binoculars. It had a number of large outbuildings. One in particular caught Terry's eye. It was near the back of the main house. It was large, had no windows, and only one door on the end facing the road. The two Russians were at the front of the main house, and didn't have a line of sight view to the door of the outbuilding that was slowly opening. He sat up straighter, then got out of the car and leaned on the hood with the glasses. Two women were leaving the outbuilding in a crouch.

"Shit." He hit redial. "Dan, get here faster."

"What's happening."

"Just get here faster and keep an eye peeled for two girls on the side of the road. I'm going to distract the help."

"Jesus."

"Yeah."

Terry jumped in the car and made a show of it leaving the shoulder. He revved the engine and left little strips of rubber behind him. As he got level to the driveway he rolled down his window and leaned his head out. "Hey, you fucking Russkies. Wanna go again?"

They started running toward him, then veered off to their car.

He saw Sophia and Kelly slowly stand. He made sure the Russians couldn't see him and waved them off, pointing back up the road, gesticulating wildly at them.

As soon as the Russian's car started he floored the accelerator, keeping their attention. Then took off with them in pursuit.

Andy leaned forward. "Who was that?"

"Terry. Found the girls. Sit back."

Andy pushed Kat to one side and leaned farther forward looking through the windscreen from the back seat.

"I said sit back." He wrenched the wheel around a corner then dramatically slowed. Mac was right behind him and came perilously close before he slowed also. The farmhouse was up and to the right. Dan saw what Terry meant. It was a perfect location. He crossed the centreline and stopped on the shoulder as a car spat out of the driveway and turned away from them in pursuit of what Dan could only assume was Terry.

He got out of the car and stood on the running board with his binoculars. Watched the scrub for bushes moving contrary to the prevailing winds.

Andy crawled out of the back seat and started walking into the bush.

"Hold up, mate. You're in no shape."

"Piss off."

"Daddy!" Kelly ran out of the bush and jumped her father, staggering him. Sophia was close behind.

Andy's eyes filled. "Oh, my God." He hugged Kelly and opened his arms to bring Sophia into the hug also, standing on the side of the road, rocking with emotion. "you two are drenched. What happened?"

Dan face split with a huge smile. "Where are the others?"

Sophia disengaged, kissing her husband on the cheek. She pointed at the outbuilding. "In there. We can't do anything for them right now. They're out of it. Drugged. An opioid, I think."

"How did you get out?"

"Mama knows how to pick locks."

Andy looked at the outbuilding for a long second. "Mac, take us back to your office."

"I agree. Kat, Stew and I are going to catch up with Terry and give him a hand. No arguments. Go."

They bundled into Mac's car, Kelly in the front, Andy and Sophia in the back. Mac pulled a U-turn and headed back toward his office.

"Get in. Let's go." Dan held the back door for Kat. "Don't jump into the fray unless you're 100% sure."

"One hundred," she replied with a grin.

Chapter Thirty-Four

The Russians were gaining on Terry's car, and there was nothing Terry could do about it. His wreck was pushed to the limit. "Hey, Siri. Redial on speaker."

He cornered and his phone skittered across the passenger seat. He lunged and grabbed it before it fell between the seat and the door and propped it up in a cup holder in the console.

"It's Dan. We got them. Where are you?"

"I have no idea. Track my phone. I'm making every left turn I come to, but I'm starting to run out of options. And I can't go off-road. There's too much of a ditch."

"I just saw them. About half a klick ahead. Pull onto the shoulder. We're right behind you."

Kat, in the front passenger seat, cracked her knuckles. "I really want to end these people once and for all."

Stew chuckled. "You frighten me, little girl."

"You have no idea."

Terry pulled off the road and the Russians followed. Before they were out of their car Stew drove his Mazda into the driver's door, slamming it shut with Vasily's right leg sticking out. The scream was immense.

Ilya jumped from the passenger side and was lining up on Terry when Kat jumped him from behind, an arm around his throat and both legs around his waist. Distracted, he didn't get a change to parry the jab Terry threw at his face, breaking his nose. He staggered backward against his car, catching Kat between him and it.

"Son of a BITCH that hurt." She locked her arm around his neck and squeezed as hard as she could, holding on as he struggled. He slowly sank to the ground, Kat still pinned between him and his car. She held on until he slumped sideways.

Terry watched him fade. He reached out and tapped her arm when Ilya was unconscious. "You can stop. Or you'll kill him."

"So maybe I shouldn't stop."

"Oh, you should."

Dan and Stew dragged Vasily to the side of the road. He sat up, leaning back on his arms.

Stew kicked him in the ribs. "What should we do with these two?" The scrawny Russian's right trouser leg was soaked with blood. His face was bruised and he was breathing heavily.

"You will die for this."

"Oh, shut up. It's over. I'm happy to cave your head in with a crowbar, but my colleagues probably wouldn't go for it," said Kat.

Dan looked around at the surroundings. They were on a small side road, with virtually no traffic. Gum trees lined both sides of the road. He smiled. "They both go in their boot and we push the car off the road. It'll be a while before anyone finds them."

"Dead, I promise you."

Stew hit him with a hard right, knocking him out. "Shit, the guy's head is concrete." He opened the boot of the car and tried lifting the big one under his arms. "Need a hand here."

Dan grabbed the legs and Terry grabbed him under the arms. They threw him in the boot, shoved his arms and legs around to make him fit, then threw Vasily in on top of him. His right leg had an extra bend in it.

Terry reached in and put the car in neutral. He, Stew and Mac got behind the car while Kat reached through the broken driver's window to steer. They got it to the edge of the embankment and let it go, watching the car bounce over the rocks, three metres to the bottom.

"That's do. Let's get back to Mac's."

Stew looked at the front left fender of his car, where he had smashed into the Russians' car. He grabbed the bottom of it and gave it a great pull. The panel moved far enough away from the tyre to allow clear passage.

"Terry, you and Kat follow me, okay? I'm not sure my car is going to make it back."

"The rest of the girls," said Kat.

Dan took a deep breath and let it out slowly. "I know. We'll regroup at Mac's and pull a plan together. Quickly. Trust me, we'll get them all back. We can't do it now. We're not prepared to handle a couple of dozen drugged girls."

Jason found the car at the bottom of the shallow ditch, the Russians in the boot. Neither one of them concious. He left them there and got back in his ute.

"What happened?"

He looked at Rhonda and scowled. "How in the hell am I supposed to know that? What a cluster." He hit speed dial 1 on his phone.

Prescott answered almost immediately. "What happened?"

"Like I'd know. Number fifteen and her mother are missing. I think the bloody Russians forgot to drug them and lock the door."

"Are the rest of them there?"

"Yeah. I locked the place down. They're all spaced out. Not going anywhere."

"What about the two idiots?"

"Both of them are in the boot of their car, in a ditch, and they have been seriously thumped. I've left them there. You might want to send someone to clean up that mess. I ain't touching it."

"Move the girls. That place has been compromised. Back track. It should be good."

Prescott hung up. Squeezed his phone as hard as he could, then launched it across the room. He missed the wall he was aiming for and it sailed through the door. Christophe grabbed it out of the air.

"Dammit, mate. You go through too many phones."

"Give me that damned thing."

"You going to throw it again?"

Prescott snatched it from Christophe's hand. "We need to move them again. Alert everyone who needs to be alerted that we're holding the sale and auction at the original location tomorrow night."

"It was attacked earlier today."

"Yeah, I heard. Some girl threw a rock at the house. Get the window fixed and up the level of security. Get some private hands on board for tomorrow's event."

"When do you want them shifted?"

"Right bloody now." He waited until Christophe left, then placed a call.

"What? This line isn't secure."

Prescott took a deep breath. "Call me back."

The call disconnected and Prescott looked at his phone like he wanted to launch it into space. He pulled his arm back to throw it when it rang. An unrecognised landline.

"Prescott."

"Had to get to a payphone. What in the hell are you calling me about?"

"We have a quality control problem. I've been paying you to cover my back for years. And it's all falling to shit. The girl we had just retrieved, along with her mother, have just been snatched again. Two of my men are out of commission, probably permanently. I've had to move the sale back to the original location because I've run out of bloody options. I'm almost positive this is all because of that PI crew in Campbelltown. I thought you had them under your thumb. What am I paying you for?"

"Watch it, mate. I could tank you and your whole organisation with a quick phone call."

"You'd be dragged down with me. And if you think a cop has a hard time behind bars, how do you think a paedo-cop would do? Enough threats. Fix this. Cut their legs off."

There was silence on the line for a few seconds.

"Okay. It's tomorrow, right?"

"Yes."

"I suggest you take four or five months off after that. Let it cool down. I'll send them in the wrong direction. Should tie them up for a couple of days at least. I'll find some sacrificial dupe and point them at him."

Prescott nodded. "You do that." He hung up, pacing in his lounge room, his blood pressure rising with every step he took.

Ryan called Peters. "Hey, mate. Can you set up a meeting with that PI joint in Campbelltown? I think they're due an update on how our investigations are going."

"Sure. They said they wanted to talk to you. Send me what time frames are good for you and I'll set something up. An hour enough?"

"Plenty. I'll wait for your call. But it needs to be today."

Chapter Thirty-Five

Ryan went through his files of known offenders. He needed someone big enough to convince his targets that he was involved in trafficking and not just a creep, but not so large as to have enough legal representation to get him out of an arrest.

And they had to be as far away from Prescott as possible.

He found a couple of candidates. Printed off their profiles.

His phone rang. Peters. "We got a time?"

"In two hours. But not in Campbelltown. They've set up base on the Central Coast. A small PI up there. I'll text you the address."

"No, they have to come down here."

"I can pass that on to them, but Dan McGinnis was pretty adamant that they were operating up there for the next few days. If you want it down here it'll have to be the day after tomorrow."

He pushed back from his desk. Picked up the profiles and slid them into his laptop bag. "Send me the address. Jesus Christ, this is insane."

"On its way. I'll join you there."

"Not necessary."

"I'll be there anyway. Andy is a friend of mine."

"Why are we wasting our time listening to this lying sack of shit?" Kat paced Mac's small office. "We know where the girls are. We need to go back and get them."

Dan shook his head. "They're moving them now. Scooping them up while they're on the move is impossible. We need to find where they're going and maybe this 'lying sack of shit' can drop a hint or two." He checked the time. "He'll be here in ten minutes. Andy, Sophia, Kelly, go back through that door. Keep it shut, and keep quiet."

"Yeah, sorry," said Mac. "That's the apartment side of my office. It's not the neatest."

Sophia shepherded her daughter through the door. "We'll be fine. Thanks."

Kat waited until the door was closed. "And that's another thing. Why is he coming to us? And at this hour? These are meetings usually held at their offices. During normal office hours."

"We're getting close to shutting this down. We suspect he's involved. This confirms it."

She kicked at Mac's desk. "Fine."

"Easy on the furniture. It might not be much, but it's all I've got." He got up from behind his desk. "We should clear some space for the guy."

Kat sighed. "Someone stay between him and me. We let him spout his crap and see if we can get anything from him."

Dan held up his finger. Footfalls on the metal steps outside Mac's office. Two sets. "Okay. Let's listen to what he has to say. Maybe it'll be useful."

Peters led Ryan in. "Our Fed friend thought you should get an update on where the trafficking case is moving. Everyone knows everybody so I'll dispense with introductions and hand it over to Inspector Ryan."

Ryan half sat on the desk. Mac, Kat, Dan, Stew and Terry fanned out in front of him. "Hey, guys." Kat glared. "Sorry. And lady." He cleared his throat. "Our task force has been digging into the human trafficking thing you stumbled into. They are buried deep. You've helped immensely by catching an edge of the veneer protecting them and pulling it back. It's given us insight into their operations and some leads to work with."

"Glad we could be of assistance," said Dan. "How far have you gotten? We'd really like to nail this prick. One of our own is wrapped up in this."

"That's right. How is Andy?"

"Tell us what you've found so far."

Ryan nodded. "Absolutely. We can confirm a shipment of twenty-two Cambodian girls were transported through the cargo facility at Port Kembla."

"Knew that already."

"You suspected. We confirmed. This was out of character for them. They usually come through Newcastle. They were moved north, as a diversion, then recently we believe they've been moved south in preparation for an auction tomorrow evening."

"South?" Kat raised an eyebrow. "You sure?"

Ryan nodded. "All indications say that. Sorry to tell you, but it seems like you've been looking in the wrong direction."

Kat sniffed. "Who's behind this? There is obviously a ringleader calling the shots. How close are you to getting him. Or her?" She glanced at Dan.

Ryan grimaced. "Very elusive character. It would certainly be someone we've had run ins with in the underage sexual abuse world in the past, and it appears they've expanded their operations." He brandished one of the file folders he'd brought with him. "This is the likely candidate. A creep by the name of John Horton. Has a spread just outside Batemans Bay."

"That's four hours south of here," said Kat.

"It is. And we believe he'll be holding an auction there tomorrow night. I've got a task force team prepping to crash the place just as it starts." He held up an index finger. "Strictly confidential. Word gets out and they'll move. Again. They were up here, but we've received intelligence that they are shuttling the girls south. If we had more information we'd intercept the shipment, but we don't."

Dan closed his eyes and took a deep, steadying breath. "Okay, what's the address at Batemans Bay?"

Ryan flipped open the file and placed it on Mac's desk. "I really shouldn't tell you. Operational security and all that. Give me a minute with Peters over here to chat about it." He steered Peters to the far side of the room, leaving the file on the desk.

Kat looked at Dan and shook her head, disgusted. She took a picture of the top sheet with her phone and rolled her eyes. "This is seriously bush league. I can't even do this anymore." She pulled the door open. "I'll be at The Pelican."

Ryan watched her leave. "Hey, what's eating her?"

"I think she's upset we were led on a wild goose chase. Four hours is a long drive."

"It's more like almost five," said Peters. "Didn't want to correct her earlier."

Stew closed the file and handed it back to Ryan. "Thanks for the debrief. You should go. We've got plans to make."

"Sure thing. Safe travels. Just don't get in our way, okay?"

Mac held the door while they left. Closed it firmly behind them. "Raise your hand if you believe the piece of shit?"

"I'm going to go get Kat before she kills someone," said Terry.

"The auction is tomorrow at the latest," said Dan. "If we're going to move the girls, we need a plan, and that plan needs to include something to offset the effects of the opioids. Stew, can you call your doctor friend and tell her what's going on? We'll need three dozen doses. See if she can get them. I'll pay for them if I have to."

Dan looked at Mac with a small smile. "Sorry to bring your ex into this, but it can't be helped. Let's get dinner."

Chapter Thirty-Six

Jane pulled a chair from an adjoining patio table and sat with Dan, Stew Andy and Mac. "Just like old times."

Kelly, Sophia, Kat and Terry were at the table next to them.

Jane lifted a bag onto the table. "Fifty doses of Narcan. Twenty pre-loaded syringes and thirty nasal sprays. On me. Where are the girls?"

"Thanks for coming up, Doc. I really appreciate it," said Kat. "We're down to two places. The big place at Avoca, or the spooky place at Wamberal. Both are large. We're split. We hit Avoca already. They led us there to fake us out so they could grab our girls. It would be a head fake for them to go back there, but maybe they think they're clever. The Wamberal house, on the other hand, is a little farther away, but appears to be bigger. We haven't been inside it."

"I wish we had grabbed one of those Russians. I'm pretty sure I could have gotten the big one to talk." Stew cracked his knuckles. "Almost positive."

"Two Russians? One big, one meth-skinny?" Jane looked from Stew to Dan. "Is that who you're talking about?"

"Why?"

"Two unidentified males, with Russian sounding accents, one big, one scrawny, were dropped off at the Gosford A&E. Ten minutes from here. They were in terrible shape. You could ask them some questions."

Mac smiled. "I missed the development of this phase of your personality."

"They'll be drugged, " said Stew. "Useless for a couple of days."

Jane smiled and rested her hand on the bag of Narcan. Pushed the bag slightly in Stew's direction.

Mac got it first. "Oh, shit. Who are you and what have you done with Jane? Never mind. I don't want to know what you did with her. I like this version."

Stew gave him a look. "Steady on, Mac."

"There are pre-teen girls being sold into sex slavery. I'd take a knife to them if I knew of a way of doing it without getting caught." Jane took a breath. "So, I can get you into the hospital room, but I can't be there when you do whatever you do. I need some level of deniability."

Dan sat back in his chair. "I don't know." He scratched his jaw. "I can't ask any of you to do this. It's too risky." He held up his hand. "Kat, stop. I know what you'd do. But I can't let it happen. I'll go in on my own. The rest of you figure out two extraction plans, one for each house. We're going to do this tonight." He looked at his watch. "Four hours to midnight."

"And if they aren't forthcoming?"

Dan looked at the table for a second. "Then we need to run both plans. Means two vans, and half the team at each location. They better be forthcoming because that's a recipe for disaster."

Jane parked in the employee parking spot at the Gosford hospital and tossed her Campbelltown Hospital staff parking pass on the dash. She reached into the carry bag in the back seat and gave Dan four syringes. "There's enough in here to strip the effects of opioids from a fully dosed elephant. The syringes are preloaded. They'll each have at least one IV. This works fastest intravenously, so find the injection port and dump the lot of it in. In less than thirty seconds the pain relief effect of the opioid will be gone. The pain will be excruciating." She scowled. "With any luck. If they've got their wits together they'll start jacking up the morphine, but it has a hard limit. If it seems like the morphine is working, dump another syringe into them. You got it?"

"Remind me to never make you angry."

They got out of the car. Jane was in a doctor's white jacket. She reached for one from the back seat and handed it to Dan. "It'll be a little tight, so don't button it up. Wait a couple of minutes after I go in. I'll get the room number they're in and text you. Go straight there. Act like you belong."

"That part I can do." He split the four syringes, two in each coat pocket. "I won't be long. I'll meet you back here. If this gets squirrely, just go."

She smiled, nodded and walked into the A&E entrance.

Dan leaned against the car, waiting. There was a steady stream of foot traffic in and out of the emergency department. Good, for him. Easier to slip in without drawing unwanted attention.

His phone chimed. Jane sent him the room number. Both Russians were in the same room.

He adjusted his collar and strode in with the imperious attitude of a doctor who deigned to spend some of his valuable time in a small regional hospital.

The room was on the second floor. He walked past the nurses' station without pausing, into the room, and closed and locked the door. Ilya was in the near bed. Vasily was on the other side of a privacy curtain, closer to the window. Ilya struggled to sit upright. Dan reached across his bed and triggered the morphine pump until his eyes closed. "Good night, big guy."

He pulled the curtain aside. "Good afternoon, Vasily. How's the leg?" He smashed his hand down on the Russian's right shin.

He groaned. "Piss off, you piece of shit. I'm going to kill you."

Dan slid the full syringe into the injection port. "One chance to do this the easy way. The girls are being moved. Because you and your flabby friend screwed up. Are they being taken to Avoca or Wamberal?"

"Get stuffed, I think you say."

Dan depressed the plunger, then pressed down on the Russian's right shin. It took about fifteen seconds before his eyes grew large and the heart rate monitor peaked.

"How about now?"

Vasily clenched his teeth and groaned. Spittle sprayed onto his chin. He hit the morphine button repeatedly and rapidly. "Get fucked."

Dan let go of Vasily's leg and slid another syringe into the injection port. He held his thumb over the plunger. "Blink once for Avoca, twice for Wamberal, three times if you'd like more pain." He depressed the plunger a millimetre. "You've got three seconds."

"What are you injecting into me. Poison?"

Dan shrugged. "If you say so. I've got two more after this. I pump them all into you and you won't be able to think straight for the next six hours. Talk. To. Me." He waited for three seconds. "Okay." He slowly depressed the plunger, his eyes locked with Vasily. "Tough, are you?"

The Narcan hit Vasily's system and Dan pressed down on his leg. "Two more, comrade."

A vein on the Russian's forehead was throbbing and his face was a claret colour. "Okay, okay. Okay. Avoca. Wamberal doesn't have the right layout. If they're moving them, it's to Avoca." His eyes widened. "Just stop it."

Dan continued depressing the plunger. "What was that? I couldn't hear you." He emptied the cylinder, tossed the syringes in the sharps disposal can and left, Vasily groaning in pain behind him.

Jane was leaning against her car. "Was going to give you maybe one more minute, then bug out. How'd it go?"

"That stuff work exactly like you said it would. Vasily is going to be a very uncomfortable man for however long it takes two doses to wash through his system. Avoca. The girls are at Avoca." He got in the car. "Let's get back to Mac's. Thanks a million."

Chapter Thirty-Seven

Dan and Jane walked into an argument in Mac's office.

"We kill them. These rat fucks don't deserve to live." Kat had staked out her position and wasn't budging.

"We get the girls, tank the dirty cop and let the rest of law enforcement sort things out. We aren't executioners. I've got to stay up here after you all leave."

Dan rested a hand on Kat's shoulder. "I know why you feel the way you do, but our main objective is to get the girls. We'll let the other chips fall where they may." He clapped his hands together. "We've got the location. They're at the Avoca property. You have a plan?"

Stew pulled the Avoca map to the top of the pile on Mac's desk.

"Makes sense. Validates the conclusion we came to. The Wamberal property has too many bottlenecks if the buyers have to bug out in a hurry."

He pointed at the house in question. "Kat managed to get the architectural drawings for this house from the council. And we have a little bit of familiarity with it, fortunately. There's a large room downstairs, like a basement, where the girls will be held and prepped. A couple of large showers, here and here where they'd clean them up prior to the sales. They'll be in that room tonight. We go in late. I expect security will be a bit tougher than we've seen anywhere else."

Dan nodded. "A distraction might pull some of them away, but Prescott will make sure the girls aren't left unattended. That's our biggest problem."

"We thought so, too," said Mac. "We need to get a couple of us in with the girls early, before the big distraction. When the shit hits the fan they'll send a couple of muscle heads in to check on the girls and we'll be there to surprise them."

Dan nodded. "The distraction?"

Sophia raised her hand. "Andy, Kelly and I are going to drive up to the house, let them know who we are and then leave very quickly."

"That's kinda dangerous."

"We'll be driving to a place where a few of Mac's friends will be waiting. Big friends."

Mac smiled. "A footy team of strapping young lads in need of a workout."

"Good. With the place clear we let Terry, Kat and Jane in to Narcan the girls, then we clear out. What's the status of the bus?"

"It'll be at the house. They had to transport the girls there."

"If it's not?"

"Mac and I are going to drive by in a few minutes to make sure," said Terry. "If it is, I'll grab it. If it's not there, we'll find one on the way back."

Dan nodded. "So go and check. We'll be doing this late at night, so everyone find somewhere to rest. Grab some food."

An hour later Terry and Mac entered the office. "The bus is acquired and hidden in Avoca."

"Good. Grab some food. Jessie brought a bunch over from The Pelican. Andy and Sophia are in the bedroom, 'resting'. Grab a piece of floor and catch some shuteye." Dan checked his watch. "We leave here in three hours."

It was overcast. The approach to the Avoca house from the dunes was in almost total darkness.

Dan motioned for Stew and Mac to get down, then pointed at a shadow he'd seen move. Someone was stationed at the back door.

Stew nodded. He handed his pack of bugs to Dan, pointed at Mac, and then to his right. Mac nodded and moved away. Stew moved forward slowly, crouched, waiting for Mac.

Who timed it perfectly.

Loud crashing in the scrub to Stew's right diverted the guard's attention. Stew launched himself from about 2 metres away, slamming the guard's head into the side of the house. He eased the guard to the ground, zip-tied his hands and gagged him.

Dan appeared beside him. "Didn't kill him, did you?"

Mac appeared alongside, looked at the form on the ground and kicked him in the head. "Who cares?"

"Gloves, everybody," whispered Stew.

Dan crouched by the back door with a lock pick set. He breached the deadbolt and eased the door open. It was dark. He turned on the torch and held his hand over it, diffusing the light. He led them to the back of the room to a set of stairs down a level.

"We didn't bug down here," whispered Stew. He stopped in front of a door at the bottom of the stairs. Checked the door knob.

It turned.

He pushed the door open into a large room with eleven bunkbeds. The girls were all asleep. "Drugged." Dan shone the light around the spacious room. "We leave them drugged until we take out the guards. Makes it easier. I'll wait by this door, you two look for any other entrance and cover them." He slid his phone out of his back pocket. "I'll let Andy know to start his moves. We've got a couple of minutes. Keep the lights off."

Stew collected his bag of listening devices and planted one in each corner of the room, two in electrical outlets and two in air vents. Then he joined Mac by the other entrance. "Good to go."

Dan settled in against the wall beside the doorknob side of the door. He pulled up his sleeve and checked the time. "Get ready. In a couple of minutes.'

The house was solid brick, double shell on the outside and concrete cladded single brick interior walls. Sound did not travel well. But they still heard the yelling when Andy pulled up to the front of the house. The door beside Dan pushed open and a hand hit the light switch. Dan pushed up with all of his strength and delivered an uppercut that snapped the recipient's head back into the brick wall and dropped him.

Mac had the other man in a choke hold from the back.

Stew watched with a smile. "One each."

Dan sent a message and a few seconds later Kat and Jane came through the door by Mac and Dan.

"How much time do we have?" Jane asked.

"Unless an army of fifty chased Andy, my guys will tie them up for hours. But we don't know what reinforcements will be coming so let's make it snappy." Mac held out his hand. "How does this work?"

Jane looked at her ex. "We'll use the nasal spray. Faster, and I won't need to train any of you to use the needles." She handed half a dozen to Mac. "Peel the back off the pack. Slip the delivery end into a nostril and depress the plunger completely. That's one full dose. They should be fully awake in about two minutes."

"How long does it last?"

"No way of knowing. Depends on the dose they had. We'll need to get them on the bus as fast as we can. Where is it?"

Dan held up his phone. "Terry is parked outside the back door. Let's go."

With five of them administering the drug, all the girls were conscious and somewhat alert in about five minutes. Dan and Stew went ahead to make sure the route to the bus was clear.

When the bus was full he pulled Terry to one side. "Take them back to The Pelican."

"It's nearly 2 in the morning, mate. They won't be open."

"They will," said Mac. "I've sorted it. They'll feed the girls. Jane will make sure they're all healthy."

"And we'll call the cops, right?"

"Not yet. We're not finished. Go. Don't stop for anyone."

The bus left with Terry, twenty-one pre-teen Cambodian girls, Jane and Kat. Stew clapped Dan on the shoulder. "That felt good. Now what?"

"Now we wrap it all up." He took a disposable pre-pay phone from his pocket, consulted a scrap of paper, and made a call.

"Who is this? Do you know what time it is?"

"Good morning, Prescott."

"Who is this? How did you get this number?"

Dan smiled and put the phone on speaker. "You're going to have a very long today, Prescott. Enjoy it. I expect it will be the last one you have as a free man. I have your girls."

Dan hung up and dropped the phone on the driveway. Smashed it repeatedly with the heel of his boot. "That transmitter still transmitting, Stew?"

"It appears so." Stew opened an app on his phone. Eight audio sources were shown as live. He adjusted a couple of settings. "Hot, and now they are being stored on the cloud."

"Perfect. Back to The Pelican for a very late dinner. Or an extremely early breakfast."

Chapter Thirty-Eight

Prescott stood stunned, looking at the phone in his hand. He'd been out almost two hours, deep into REM sleep, when his phone rang, and he wasn't sure what was real and what was a dream. He called the head of the team watching the Avoca house.

It rang out to voicemail.

"Son of a bitch." He made another call. "Jason, meet me at the Avoca house, now."

"Bloody hell. Do you know what time it is?"

"Now!"

He hung up and made another call. "Timothy Ryan, you useless son of a bitch."

"Prescott? It's two in the fucking morning."

"You shit stain. I'm texting you an address in Avoca. Be there in less than an hour. You will lead the investigation into where my girls went."

"I don't work - what? You lost them ALL?"

"I just sent the address. You've got an hour to come up with some lame-arsed excuse for your MONUMENTAL INCOMPETENCE."

He threw the phone on his bed and got dressed. Then made one last call.

"Boss, it's almost 2:30. What in the hell is wrong with you?"

"Avoca house, Christophe. Now. I've been told all the girls have been taken. I can't reach any of the security team. I'm on my way. Need you there to discuss next steps, particularly with our clients."

"We've taken over $800,000 for those girls in pre-payments."

"I can do the maths. Meet me there."

When Prescott arrived Ryan was sitting in his car in the drive. He could see Jason's truck and Christophe's car. He rapped on Ryan's window. "Get out of the car."

The Fed rolled down his window. "I'm not going in there. It's a crime scene."

Prescott squatted by the window, his grin a rictus of revulsion. "I'm not going to call the cops, idiot. Just you. You will look around, use whatever resources you have to find out who did whatever happened here, then give the information to me. Jason will do the rest."

Ryan sat there, unmoving.

Prescott leaned closer. "Move it," he hissed. "I have pictures of you with a twelve year old girl doing things that will get you 25 years in a maximum security prison. Except you probably wouldn't last 25 hours. Go." He stood and opened the car door, holding it for Ryan.

Jason was downstairs. He had a depleted Narcan nasal spray device in his hand. He threw it at Ryan when he saw him. "They came prepared. This was an organised hit. It wasn't some fluke escape. Protection? Like a condom with a bloody great hole ripped in it." He pointed at the Narcan device at his feet. "Can you get anything from that thing that would help you find out who did this, or do I just rip your bloody arms off now and beat you to death with them?"

"Obviously your operational security sucked. And you know who did this. You took one of their daughters. And then the wife. I can't help you if you run a shithouse operation."

Jason curled his hand into a fist and leaned in close to Ryan's face. "So help me God, I will make you hurt in ways you haven't even imagined."

"If it wasn't for me, you pommy bastard, you and your chippy bitch would be in jail by now."

Prescott watched the tension build. On any other day he'd let Jason slowly kill the cop, but he still needed him. "Break it up. You'll get your chance, Jason. Ryan, do what you do and get this resolved, and my girls back to me by NOON AT THE LATEST." He checked his watch. "That's eight hours. Find them. Bring them back."

He turned to Jason. "You. You find the rest of this - what did Ryan call it? - shithouse security team and bring them all to me. Here. I'll deal with them myself."

The owners of The Pelican had put ten tables together in the middle of the restaurant. The girls sat around them, slowly realising that they were free. Jessie, with Kat's assistance, was bustling around like she had 22 younger sisters, leaving plates of chicken and chips evenly space along the table. Sophia and Kelly were moving from seat to seat, leaning between the girls reassuring them that they were safe. And that they should eat.

Dan, Terry and Stew sat together. Andy was at a separate table in deep conversation with Mac.

Stew watched Jessie and the girls and smiled. "This is nice. It feels good when we win one."

"We're not finished." Dan stretched. "They've got a long road ahead of them. They'll be feeling the after effects of opioid use for months. We need to get back to our office. Final nail." He leaned over and tapped Andy on the arm. "We're heading back. You stay up here with your wife and daughter. Take a break. We've got it from here."

Andy smiled. "I was just talking to Mac. He's got contacts in immigration. He'll start working with them tomorrow to get the girls back home. We'll hang around and help with translations."

Dan looked at the girls, starting to come out of the drugged stupor and digging into the food. "They're going to need medical care. I'm going to finish this tomorrow. I'll let you know when. Keep the girls under cover. I don't want Prescott getting any ideas." He patted Andy on the arm. "Only one day. It'll be good by tonight." He tapped the table. "The rest of us are heading back to the home office."

He stopped by Kat on the way out. "You can stay here for a couple of days or come back to the office with us and help us end it. Your choice."

She hugged Jessie. "I'll be back up some day. You can teach me how to kite surf." She gave Dan a bit of a push. "Let's go end these creeps."

Chapter Thirty-Nine

Beryl had coffee ready when they returned. She look pointedly at her watch as they trudged in. "Welcome back. It's 6 am. When's the last time any of you slept?"

"Feels like months," said Stew.

"I had the whole back seat of Terry's car to sleep. I'm ready to go." Kat dropped her bag on the table in the kitchen and poured a cup of coffee. "Someone just needs to point me in the right direction."

Dan grabbed a cup and sat at his desk. He opened his phone and scrolled through his contacts, then called.

"Peters speaking. What in the hell are you doing, calling me at this hour?"

"I disturb you?"

"What do you want, McGinnis?"

"Contact your Fed friends and set up a meeting with us in his offices, as soon as possible, today, so we can give them an update on the sex trafficking operation they're investigating."

"You've made some progress?"

"Critical info to share." Dan yawned. "Ryan has to be there. He's going to make an excuse. Probably two. He *needs* to be there. And you need to have enough people on hand in case it gets nasty when you arrest him."

"What?"

"Text me the address and the time. I've got a presentation to put together."

"Hang on. Arrest?"

"Make sure he's there, Wazza." Dan cut the call and nudged Stew who was resting his head on the table. "Mate, check the recordings. Get some juicy clips ready."

Stew arched back, stretching and yawning. "I'm going to sleep for a week when we're finished with this. You know, kinda pissed nobody is paying us for this. We've put in a ton of work. And it's not like we'll be getting our bugs back."

Kat smiled. "I've got an idea about that. Might need a little bit of help from Terry." She chuckled. "I could use a new pair of boots."

"Stew, the recordings. Kat, be careful."

"Always."

Stew pushed away from the table, accepted the offer of a mug of coffee from Beryl and sat in front of his computer. "Dan-o, I'll send you half a dozen clips, as clear as I can get them. With subtitles and names where I know them. Give me an hour."

"Works for me. Anyone not doing something, rest. It's going to be a long day."

"It's already been a long day."

Dan and Stew passed through security at the AFP offices on Goulburn Street in Sydney. Collected their laptops and cell phones on the other side of the magnometer and met Warren Peters. In plain clothes.

"No uniform, Wazza?"

"Not officially on duty. But I'll have a team in the room, like you suggested. I have to admit, my curiosity is piqued."

Dan clapped hm on the shoulder. "Lead the way. This is going to be fun."

The meeting was in a large boardroom. Dan and Stew were the last to arrive. In addition to a couple of suits who looked just like local cops in suits was Tim Ryan, looking even more tired than Dan felt, and a woman with a look that approximated a mixture of bored, curious and annoyed.

"You must be the gentlemen Mr Peters insisted we meet." She stood and extended her hand. "I'm Tilda Harrington, I run the Australia Centre to Counter Child Exploitation. Ryan is here also. Apparently you have an update on the case he's currently working?"

Dan shook her hand. "Very nice to meet you. I'm Dan McGinnis, this is Stewart Edwards, of McGinnis Investigations. Yes, we have an update." He sat and opened his laptop. "Can we connect to the monitor and speakers?"

Ryan cleared his throat and stood. "I stopped by their operations on the Central Coast yesterday and let them know we believed there's an auction going on somewhere in Batemans Bay this afternoon. I really should be heading there now."

"I think you should stay for this talk," said Harrington. "In fact, I insist."

Ryan slowly sat. "Sure."

"Please proceed, Mr McGinnis."

Dan stood. "This whole mess came to our attention when we found one of our colleagues, Andy Smith, near death, lying in a pool of his blood in our office kitchen. It ended last night when we liberated twenty-one underage girls from a house on Avoca Beach." He stared at Ryan. "This is despite the fact we'd been told by *Agent* Ryan that we were looking in the wrong place, and that we'd be better off travelling five hours south on a wild goose chase."

He hit a key on his laptop. A collage of the houses, grabbed from Google Earth, filled the screen. "These are the properties owned by Sam Prescott, or one of his legal entities." He slid a folder over to Harrington. "Proof he owns these properties."

Harrington leaned forward. "Can we go back to the liberated children? Where are they now?"

"A colleague of mine is working with the Royal Cambodian Embassy in Canberra to find their families and repatriate them.

They're safe. I'll get to them in a minute. Back to the properties."

"So what?" said Ryan. "Prescott is wealthy. I'd be surprised if he *didn't* own that many homes."

"He's not careful. Search these properties and I'll guarantee you in at least four of them you'll find more than a little forensic evidence of those girls."

Ryan leaned back in his chair. "I don't know what kind of training you need to go through to get a PI licence, but we can't just search a place. We need reasonable suspicion that a particular circumstance or fact exists for us to conduct a search. Your say-so doesn't cut it."

"We'll get to that, too." He tapped another key on his laptop. A collage of faces filled the screen, Prescott in the middle.

"These are the people we've come across in our investigation. Prescott in the middle, obviously. The man and woman on the left are Jason and Rhona. Prescott's muscle. They put Andy in the hospital twice. The couple of men to the right are Russians. The tall one is Ilya and the short one is Vasily. As of yesterday they were in the hospital in Gosford. They talk a mean story, but a 60 kilo, 25-year-old woman on my team took out the big one."

He tapped another key. Ryan's face appeared above Prescott's.

"What in the hell is this?"

"Sit down, Ryan." Dan had steel in his voice. "We were wondering why we were always a step behind. Then someone on my team caught Ryan having a nice, friendly with a known child offender, just after the offender's case was tossed due to lack of evidence." He tapped a key and a picture of Ryan with Leong Chang

Yu slid over the rest of the photos.

"We've known about you for a couple of days, Ryan. Believe me, if Kat was here she would beat on you until every bone in your body was broken."

Ryan stood, pushing his chair back hard enough to bounce it off the wall. "You get the hell out of here before I have you charged with obstruction of justice, and whatever else I can think of."

"Sit down, mate. I'm not done. Stew, which is the best one?"

"Clip number three."

Dan stared at Ryan. He waited until the Fed slowly sat. Stew took over the laptop and found the file. There was a hiss of static before the voices. As the audio played, subtitles showed on the screen, the voices named.

RYAN: "Obviously your operational security sucked. And you know who did this. You took one of their daughters. And then the wife. I can't help you if you run a shithouse operation."

JASON: "So help me god, I will make you hurt in ways you haven't even imagined."

RYAN: "If it wasn't for me, you pommy bastard, you and your chippy bitch would be in jail by now."

"Those are from audio devices we installed in the Avoca property. Recorded at about 3:30 this morning. The pommy bastard and his chippy bitch are the Jason and Rhonda I mentioned earlier. I've got more where that came from. A lot more." Dan slid a thumb drive across the table to Harrington. "Everything's on there. The girls are on the Central Coast, lying low today. I'll arrange for you and your team to meet them. They are going to need medical and psychological help to get past this." He pointed at Ryan. "I suggest you take his phone before he calls Prescott and warns him about what's about to come down on him."

Ryan lunged across the table at Dan and was grabbed by the two cops in suits. They relieved him of his sidearm and mobile phone and pulled his arms behind him.

Harrington watched, concern etched on her face. "This isn't good, Mr McGinnis." She held up the thumb drive. "Someone on my team is going to look at this and take it from here. I don't think we can use the audio recordings, but the photograph will be enough to get us warrants for Prescott's houses. And I will take you up on the invitation to meet these girls."

She stood. "Take Ryan to my office. Peters, thank you for bringing this to my attention. I'll keep your office across the developments. Gentlemen, thank you."

She left, Ryan with his escorts in tow.

Peters looked at Dan and Stew and shook his head. Let out a low whistle. "Wow. You know I had no idea, right?"

"Relax mate, we know." Dan smiled. "I've got to admit, that felt good. Now, I'm exhausted. It's an hour back to the office. Thanks for your help, Wazza. Let me know what they tell you. I seriously doubt they'll keep us in the loop." He handed Peters a thumb drive. "Same stuff I gave Harrington."

"Now if you'll excuse us, there's a bed calling my name." Stew closed up the laptop, stowed it in its case and handed it to Dan. "Let's go."

Andy and Sophia met the immigration representative at The Pelican. She was young, nervous and seemed a little out of her element.

"Hi. The waitress said you two are the ones I should talk to. My name is Leah Covic. I was closest to here. A delegation will be arriving tomorrow from Canberra, as well as representatives from the Royal Cambodian Embassy."

Sophia smiled. "Please, sit. Don't be so nervous. I am Sophia and this is my husband Andy. I am sure you'd like to meet the girls and make sure they are okay." She caught the worried look on Leah's face. "They are all healthy. They are suffering some from the opioids withdrawal. I can translate for you. One of them is my daughter."

Leah's eyes grew huge. "Oh my." She leaned forward. "I heard that a vigilante team rescued them and captured the people who did this."

"I couldn't say. The girls are bunking at an all-girls dorm just up the road. Would you like us to take you there now?"

Dan looked out of his office window at the billowing smoke about a block and a half away. Sirens sounded in the distance. "Nasty looking fire, Stew. Any idea what it is?"

"No." He scratched his chin. "Do you think we got all of the arseholes involved in this?"

Kat popped her head in the office, slightly out of breath. "There was at least one guy you all forgot about." She sniffed. "Don't worry. I handled it." She smiled.

Dan looked at her, then out the window again. "Shit. Are you kidding?"

She kept a smile on her face, but didn't answer. Waggled her eyebrows.

"Is he in there?"

"Is who in where?" asked Stew.

"The guy who had a very dodgy business model." Kat pulled her laptop from her bag. "Speaking of which, Terry and I found an escrow account with $811,500 in it. To which charities do you think I should distribute most of it? Hagar? Destiny Rescue? ZOE? A21? All of them? $200K each? I, personally, am getting a new pair of boots."

About the Author

Tony McFadden is a displaced Canadian now calling Australia his home. He and his wife and two children live near the beaches where he spends as much of his time as possible writing.

More about Tony and his writing can be found on the interwebs at TonyMcFadden.net/mybooks, Facebook and Twitter.

Also by Tony McFadden
G'Day LA
G'Day USA

Matt's War
Daly Battles: The Fall of Pyongyang
Target: Australia

Book 'Em - An Eamonn Shute Mystery
Unprotected Sax
Family Matters

Have Wormhole, Will Travel
Killing Time

Mac D: Private Investigator
A Step Too Far (A Mac D Case)
Hunter/Prey (A Mac D Case)

The Murder of Jeremy Brookes (A McGinnis Investigations Case)

www.ingramcontent.com/pod-product-compliance
Lightning Source LLC
Chambersburg PA
CBHW071920130726
47909CB00014B/2211